FISHING IN THE INTERCOASTAL AND OTHER STORIES
by Elaine Rosenberg Miller

TABLE OF CONTENTS

ZAYDE

My grandfather had died.

I was four years old.

I rested my elbows on my mother's knees and gazed up at the strange men.

They moved in and out of our small apartment, their heads and shoulders covered by striped shawls.

Standing closely together, they swayed and chanted in rhythmic voices.

My father had cried.

It was the first time that I had seen him cry.

I would not see him cry again until his mother died twenty years later.

To me, my father was a broad, fiercely strong man.

His grief was contained, but he cried.

"What happened?" I asked my mother.

"*Zayde* died in Israel."

Somehow, I knew that Israel was far away, this Zayde person was important to my father and that he was gone forever.

I knew something had happened.

These men were not like my relatives.

These men spoke English, not Yiddish.

My family had black numbers etched into their soft forearms.

These men were unmarked.

I looked at my mother.

She had dark hair and olive skin.

She would begin graying shortly.

I didn't know that nine years earlier she had been a prisoner in a death camp.

"One more week," she later told me, "I would no longer have lived."

She watched the men.

I did not know what she was thinking.

She was often withdrawn, as if she were observing something that could not be seen by anyone else. In my childish manner, I had once said "Sometimes, I think that you are in a club against me!"

I wasn't sure what I meant.

She patted my head.

It was one of the few times I could remember her sitting. She was forever cleaning, cooking or shopping. I was always with her.

The days came to an end.

The men departed.

My father shaved the beard that had grown on his solemn face.

He returned to work.

Life went on.

Williamsburg, Brooklyn was a slum.

We lived in a five-story tenement owned by *The Byliss,* an elderly Jewish woman.

I suppose her name was Mrs. Byliss but my mother called her "*The Byliss*". She decided to educate my mother in Americanisms. She taught her how to speak to shopkeepers, including *De Alte Yanish,* the second hand dealer. His dusty store was filled with tilted and dented pots and pans, bits of cloth and mismatched dishes. He had a fiery temper. He would take things out of my mother's hands and scream "Do me a favor. Don't buy anything here!" My mother would exit his store distressed. Still she returned, for the items she needed could be found for pennies.

The Byliss was immune to *De Alte Yanish's* curses.

When she entered his store, he stayed behind the counter.

Her white hair piled on top of her head, her stout legs pointed in opposing directions, *The Byliss* would sit on a chair next to the cool granite stoop in front of the tenement, guarding her domain.

"She looks like Shirley Temple!" she told my mother, pointing at me.

"*Vere ist Shirley Temple?*" my mother asked.

The Byliss collected our rent.

Twenty-three dollars per month.

 She would fill out a receipt in her book, tear out the page and hand it to my mother.

The Byliss had also come "from the other side" as my mother liked to say, but she had lived in Williamsburg for many years, even before the war. She would speak to my mother in Yiddish mixed with English, mangling both languages.

Our apartment had a long, dark hallway.

Neighbors on the top floor had the same apartment as ours. My sister and

I would play street games with their young daughter. Once, I peered inside their apartment through the open front door.

A rope swing was attached to the ceiling of the hallway!

A swing was an outside thing, yet here it was in their apartment!

It was not something my mother would do.

Filled with fear and curiosity, I wondered if there were other strange things that could be found in their apartment.

Perhaps a pet?

The entrance corridor in our apartment extended into the kitchen.

Immediately to the left of the kitchen was a dark bedroom where my sister and I slept. On the other side of the kitchen was the bathroom, living room and my parents' bedroom.

In the summer months, my sister and I would climb out of their bedroom window and play on the grated fire escape affixed to the outside of the building.

I would gaze at the slender trees, with their fern-like leaves struggling to grow between the cracks in the cement, the backs of other tenements, the litter, the tiny sky and think of distant things.

My parents' bedroom had shiny furniture with round, molded corners. A vertical mirror above the dresser reflected the pale blue circular patterned chenille bedspread. I would pull the puffy cotton threads and roll them into little balls and hide them in my pockets.

An overhead tank was suspended from the ceiling of the bathroom.

I would pull the metal chain to hear the roar of the rushing water.

The medicine cabinet had strange things.

Chocolate laxatives.

Band-Aids.

I once took my mother's lipstick and smeared red drawings on the yellow bathroom walls.

She cried.

"A Dollar Ninety-Eight Hazel Bishop lipstick!" she said.

But she didn't punish me.

Holes in the wall plaster were visible above the kitchen table.

I would pick at the cavities as we ate, enlarging them.

An occasional mouse would run across the floor, amusing my sister and I.

Our bedroom window faced a brick wall.

After we left our cribs, we shared a bed.

We fought, but every night I would call her name.

"What?" she would ask.

"Nothing," I would respond and then I would be able to fall asleep.

My father worked many hours.

He was a mechanic and truck driver. A year after coming to America, he bought a truck. He stored it in a nearby garage. He soon bought another truck.

Summers, he would return from work perspiring, his shirt and trousers damp. Winters, he wore a long woolen garment under his clothes. He traveled to far-off places. Washington. Baltimore. He would be gone for days. When he returned, my sister and I waited to catch his attention. He would eat the meals my mother had prepared and then turn to us. I would sit on his lap as he sang a song calling me his little kitten.

He sang in Yiddish, the language of lullabies.

Sundays, we would go to the corner restaurant.

Rising steam fogged the already darkened, navy-blue glass windows.

Embossed tin tiles covered the ceiling.

The smells of the wurst, pastrami and salami were overwhelming.

In the winter, we would hang our coats on racks. One day, I watched a woman lift my new turquoise coat with its double row of covered buttons off the wall hook and turn to leave.

"*Tatteh*," I said, as if in slow motion. "Look!"

He approached her and returned with the coat.

"*Effsuh she hot gedarft et fir ihr eigeneh kindt*," my mother said.

Red flowers in clay pots lined the entranceway to the Italian barber's shop.

A woman who lived on the first floor of our tenement was often in the shop.

She had long, wavy brown hair and wore tight clothes.

She had one son and no husband.

The son was "wild" it was said.

Once, at the barber's she insisted that I eat flat beans that he had cooked.

Being compliant, I did.

She watched me with a grin.

The beans swam in bitter, golden oil unlike anything my mother had ever made.

I wondered if they were poisoned.

Later, when I told my mother about the foreign beans, she was unhappy.

There was a stable near our apartment house.

A single horse lived in the recesses of the structure.

The animal fought with the hooded automobiles for space on the cobblestone streets.

The cars won and the horse disappeared.

My mother sewed our clothes.

She made us flowered dirndl skirts with suspenders.

Misplaced Heidis, we marched along the crumbling streets of Williamsburg.

Another time, she sewed red-dotted white organza dresses.

They itched like mad but I loved them.

We wore them with white cotton net gloves, white socks and tee-strapped white shoes.

She took us to the neighborhood photographer.

He insisted on putting red lipstick on my pale sister and me.

I smiled at the camera, arms to my side, feet parallel.

A small metal button with the number "6" was pinned to the middle of my speckled chest, a present from an aunt.

My sister slumped, her foot awkwardly turned out, her delicate neck rising from the shoulders of the torturous frock.

"I shouldn't have listened to him with the lipstick!" my mother said whenever she saw the photograph.

My parents purchased many copies and sent them everywhere, including Israel.

Years later, I found one on my grandmother's bureau.

I watched her read from her prayer book as she sat by a window overlooking the Carmel Mountains in Haifa. Photographs of other grandchildren were pressed under a glass table top but my sister and I stood apart, free and immortal.

When I had children, I send many photographs to my parents.

"You with your pictures!" my mother protested.

Later, I realized that I had done so because she had been unable to send pictures of us to her parents who had been killed during the war.

Sometimes people would ask my mother questions about the war.

She would not answer.

It was as if she had not heard them.

A young man, a policeman, patrolled our neighborhood. Whenever my mother saw him, she crossed to the other side of the street, even though it was said that he was Jewish.

We attended a nearby synagogue.

The women sat in the balcony.

I remember my father standing shoeless before an embroidered velvet curtain, his head and face covered, his arms outstretched and shout in a terrifying voice, unlike his own.

"*Ah-yi-yi-yi!*"

Other men stood beside him, hidden beneath their own shawls, joining their voices with his.

The people in the seats turned their faces away from the stage.

I rested my flushed cheek against the cold brass railing.

What was happening?

No one explained.

We played in a public park.

Spanish-speaking people began to move into Williamsburg.

"*Mira! Mira!*" the mothers screamed at their children.

The young men wore white undershirts exposing their arms and necks.

Once, to attract the attention of my father who would, from time to time hire them, one man took another by the waist and turned up upside down and placed him in a wire garbage can.

The other men whistled and clapped.

"Higher! Higher!" I would shout, my toes pointed to the sky as my father pushed the swing, but I was afraid to go too high lest I overshoot the frame and fall.

Our building had a superintendent.

Charlie had twelve children.

My mother would pay one of his daughters to walk us to school a few blocks away.

In the winter, Charlie's family would have a giant tree in their apartment.

It was decorated with shiny red and silver balls.

The tree seemed to go on and on.

Sometimes, Charlie disappeared.

His wife would cry.

He would return.

They would have more children.

One day, my father bought a television set.

Mesmerized, I sang along with Howdy Dowdy, rode with Roy Rogers and Dale Evans and their horses, Trigger and Buttermilk.

My heart leapt when Roy came through the swinging bar room doors.

Three television stations were available.

Alone and bored, I once forced a dial in the opposite direction to seek additional channels.

There must be more channels, I reasoned. Our parents just hadn't told us about them.

I heard the crack of broken plastic as the knob began to spin aimlessly around.

I loved school.

I loved the toys, the other children, the music and the games.

One day, we put on a musical performance. I held an exquisite doll with blonde, shiny curls and a lace costume and sang.

My mother sat with the other mothers.

I didn't know if she understood all the words.

It was the first time she had been in the classroom.

The sun streamed in through the tall, schoolroom windows.

She smiled at me.

After the show, the teacher took the doll away.

Its body continued to weigh heavily on my chubby arms.

I thought it had been mine to keep.

There was a Catholic orphanage across the street from our apartment building.

One day, my sister, dragging me behind her, skipped past the iron entrance gates. She wanted to play with the orphans' toys.

Late in the afternoon, neighbors told my frantic mother that my sister had run off again and she came to get us.

We refused to acknowledge her.

As we were fair haired and she was black haired, for a moment it seemed as if the nuns believed us.

Hysterically, she managed to pull us back home.

Another time, as my mother busied herself with yet another task, we decided to play hide and seek.

We chased each other around the apartment. Passing an open window we shrieked "Help!" My mother flew into the room. We hid behind the new washing machine. I watched my mother's horrified face.

"Surprise!" I shouted weakly, regretting what we had done. It took a long time for my mother to compose herself.

One day my father drove his truck to our tenement. Men came and carried away our clothing.

We left the furniture.

The Byliss waived goodbye.

I stood beside my father in the cab of the truck.

Looking over his shoulder at the swiftly passing streets, I thought, "Now my life will change forever."

THE FIREFLIES

She sat on the granite boulder, swinging her short legs.

Car after car passed on the rural highway, but none turned into the gravel roadway leading to their bungalow colony.

She wondered why her mother hadn't come to look for her.

Still, she felt grateful that she could rest in solitude.

Her mother had an anxious manner, always busy.

She wondered how she could be so busy in the country.

They were far away from the cars, the horns, the buses, the screaming children.

They were in the mountains.

Nights felt quickly and resolutely.

She never understood her mother.

Sometimes, she would see her softly crying as she sat on the slatted wooden chair, the same chair which she used to clamp a heavy steel grinder into which she would feed chunks of fresh carp. Long rows of twirled fish would flow out of the grated nozzle as she turned the handle.

She knew that her mother was unlike other mothers. She knew that something had happened to her but she was never sure what had happened. Her past was divided into "The War" and "Before the War", never talking about either.

She continued to wait.

He father spent weekdays in the city and then would drive to the mountains on late Friday afternoons. He always brought toys.

Everyone called her a "Daddy's girl".

She wasn't sure what it meant, but she knew that nothing made her happier than to please her father.

She wondered where her sister was.

They had spent the afternoon splashing in the pool. She didn't know how to swim and neither, it seemed, did anyone else. Everyone just bobbed and held onto the sides or sat on the flaking steps.

Her sister had inexhaustible energy. She played, ran, leapt, shouted and disappeared daily.

She peered down the road.

It was empty.

A small knot of anxiety began to build in her heart.

"What if....?" she thought.

The sun was setting.

Still, she sat alone.

She fingered the rock's speckled granite surface.

Last time, he had bought them matching toy plastic banjoes.

She put her hand to her mouth with joy

"He must really love us," she thought.

But no one showed them how to use the banjos. They plucked the plastic strings and soon they became loose and then, lost.

She was tired.

It had been a long day.

They had picked blueberries in the neighboring field. They had walked and walked.

She heard the sound of a cars wheels against the stones.

Headlights illuminated the road.

She stood up.

"Daddy!" she wanted to say but the car drove by.

She climbed back onto the boulder.

"If I stay here, he will have to see me," she thought.

Suddenly she saw the flicker of a light floating in the air, turning, then disappearing, then another and then another. The lights flicked on and off, creating semi-circled orbits in the darkening sunset.

"Oh," she thought. "Fireflies!"

She watched their trails turn and disappear, a dance of light and life.

"Tatteh, where are you?" she thought, almost crying.

Somehow, the fireflies made her sad, made her think of her mother's mute stare, her father's absences.

She felt a chill in the air as the sun set.

Still, her father's car did not appear, still her mother did not come to look for her.

Alone, she sat on the stone alongside the road leading into the bungalow colony and waited.

THE TASHKA

It was made of aluminum, I suppose or some other metal.

It was shiny and steel colored and had my father's other name painted in black letters on its surface, his last name first, followed by his first name, as was the European custom.

Only, it wasn't his American first name, Charles or even his Yiddish name, Shaya. It was his Polish first name, the one with the impossible, hard to pronounce consonants, *Szaje.*

My parents' multiple names were the bane of my existence.

Why couldn't they be named Richard? Nancy?

And where was my horse?

I knew that they had come from somewhere else and now, years later, I realized that they also were someone else.

They had both been small town ("*shtetl*") born Jews.

Their villages had no electricity. They drew their water from stone wells in the market place or nearby rivers.

Yet, the lives they later described were happy ones, filled with near and extended families.

But back then, I knew none of this.

I was just uncomfortable, perhaps embarrassed that my father still had a suitcase with his Polish name on it.

Everyone in summer camp had hard bodied, anonymous luggage.

My father's *tashka* screamed "refugee".

There was much about my parents that disturbed me.

I felt that they harbored secrets from my sister and I. It would be decades before I learned about my father's flight to Siberia and Central Asia and my mother imprisonment in Auschwitz and forced labor camp.

We were in summer camp in the Catskill Mountains of upstate New York, living what I thought was a typical American lifestyle.

But not quite.

It was an all-girls camp.

We were barred from wearing short-sleeved shirts or shorts. There was no pool.

There was, however a leaf filled lake, a section of which, cordoned off by ropes, we were permitted (yes, in bathing suits) to enter. There was no instruction or swimming, but there was plenty of frolicking. Adventurous (and accident-prone) I nearly drowned when I once ducked under the ropes and left the enclosed area. My feet promptly became stuck in the soggy, muck-filled lake bottom as the dark water began to lick my nose.

Somehow, after several attempts (unobserved by anyone. There was no life-guard) I managed to grab the rope and pull myself out. I could feel the the vacuum as my feet popped out of the miasma.

At home, we did not dress "modestly". We wore shorts in the summer and pants in the winter. My mother did not wear a wig like many of the other women. She wore suits and dresses and carried gloves, even when she did her shopping.

But here, in the dark piney reaches of the camp, isolated from our Brooklyn neighborhood, I was brought back to the insular, lost world of my parents.

And I found myself liking it.

"Ain't going to work on Saturday" we sang. "Double, double triple pay won't make me work on Saturday" I joined in, pounding the tables, shouting and clapping with the other girls. .

I found myself adjusting to the camp's primitive conditions (outside showers).

It once been a "union resort" (fur workers, the silverware told us) and now belonged to the Lubavitch Hasids, an outreach program that had begun in Tzarist Russia and was re-established in Brooklyn after the war

The name of the camp was "Camp Emunah".

"Emunah" meant "hope" in Hebrew.

At first, I thought that Emunah was a good name. Once there, you "hoped to get out" but after a while I began to make friends with the other girls and soon felt as if I were part of a big family, separate from my parents and relatives, but recognizable and welcoming.

A tall, red bearded rabbi was the director of the camp. His many children, most of whom were also red-headed, administered it. The highlight of the summer was being chosen to sing in the choir. Our efforts were recorded and we were told that they would be broadcast on radio.

I sang my heart out and they invited me to join the choir.

Most of the campers were from strictly religious homes but they were secular girls as well.

Camp Emunah embraced them all.

There was "Honey" a wiry, sardonic girl. Her name may have been "Chana" but in camp she was "Honey". Her parents were divorced. She was an only child. Her father was a slender man, not big or blustery or strong like my father. He was more of a friend to Honey, than a father.

My parents failed to visit us on Visiting Day.

"Where were my parents?" I demanded of the head counselor. She did not know.

I asked to use the office telephone.

I dialed "O for operator and asked her to call the numbers of several area hotels. I was repeatedly told "No one here by that name". Finally, I remembered the name of a hotel that my aunt and uncle favored and I found them.

"Where were you? You didn't come for Visiting Day!"

"We were on vacation," my father said.

Vacation?

I wasn't sure whether I liked the old parents or the new parents.

A voice within me asked "How could they have fun without me?"

Finally, camp came to an end.

I sat on the stone wall bordering the road leading to the entrance and waited.

To my great relief, they showed up, my father driving his new champagne and gold Oldsmobile Rocket 88 automobile.

They went to my room and collected my things.

Suddenly I realized that the metal suitcase was lying on the floor.

"You forgot it!" I shouted.

"Never mind," he said. "We don't want it."

I looked over my shoulder.

The *tashka* was lying askew, the ebony letters unreadable.

 I followed my parents out.

Amid squabbling and hints of inclement weather, they packed the family car and set off for the mountains.

It was the first week of summer and her father's vacation and they were going to a hotel.

As the years passed, they had progressed to larger and larger bungalows until they occupied the most deluxe model in the colony and despite the modern appliances and redwood paneling, her mother had announced that she was refusing to cook any longer any longer and that they were going to a hotel.

Deborah didn't mind. She had been bored for the last two summers, had found the screaming children annoying and the aimless walks among the dead skunks senseless and, besides, her mother had bought her and her sister new dresses and heels and stockings and her sister had been setting her own hair all winter and Deborah hoped that she would teach her how to do it as well in the country.

So, they began their trip.

They argued about opening the windows in the car. They bickered about stopping to eat. They quarreled so long that their father turned around and smacked them on their knees. Deborah tried to keep from crying for, as usual, her father had struck her first. She opened a book and tried to read. It was a mystery story about a girl kidnapped by a crime ring who managed, through her wits and courage, to escape. She read as long as she could but the motion of the car made her sick and she lay back to rest.

She watched Anna's profile against the rushing trees. Her white skin and gray blue eyes stood in repose.

"Listen, Fatso," Anna suddenly said, "when we get to the hotel, I don't want you trailing around after me. Understand?"

"What?" Deborah said, with as much disbelief as she could muster.

"You know, I don't want you embarrassing me like you did with Philip."

"That creep."

"He is not a creep. He's on the basketball team. And you'd just better shut up."

Deborah slunk back and did not say anything for the rest of the ride.

Her mother offered her oranges but she would not turn her head, so the family ate them all. Anna ate a small slice but refused to eat any more so her mother found a chocolate covered caramel in the bottom of her purse, unwrapped it and offered it to Deborah She shook her head so she gave it to her sister. Anna sat on her slim ankles and slowly licked the cube. When Deborah tried to sit as Anna sat, she felt bloated and tipsy. Her legs would fall asleep. She hadn't said anything that awful to Philip. He played at the high school where Deborah was a freshman and Anna was a sophomore. They had been riding home on the bus after a museum trip and Anna had said that she had seen a certain movie and Deborah denied it. She had not seen the movie. Deborah was certain. Anna came home and ranted and slammed doors and said she would kill Deborah and threw her colored pencils in the incinerator and Deborah threw her stuffed toy dog from Michael out the window. Anna moved towards Deborah's biographies of famous scientists but their mother rushed in stopping her, vowing to tell their father what Deborah had done.

She hadn't done anything that terrible. She had waited for a lull in the conversation and observed, gently, "No, you didn't." That was all.

She had hoped that Anna had forgotten.

They arrived at the hotel and a bellboy rushed out, pushing a clothes rack. He hung their shiny dresses and her mother's autumn haze mink stole on the horizontal pole, placed their suitcases on the platform and wheeled it into the lobby.

"Smell that air conditioning!" her father said.

Deborah trailed her family, feeling rumpled and hot.

The main room had large chandeliers suspended from the ceiling and meandering sofas upholstered in plush green fabric.

She walked around a corner and found a bespectacled boy sitting in front of a color television set, eating peanuts and watching cartoons. They looked at each other.

"We just came," Deborah said, smiling.

"Hi," the boy responded not turning from the cat and mouse chase.

"Yeah," said Deborah for no reason at all.

He looked up. "We came yesterday. How long are you staying?"

"Four weeks," she replied.

"Us, too." He had blonde hair like Anna.

'See you later," she said, smiling again.

She returned to her family who had finished checking in. The bellboy was staring at Anna.

"Yes, Mr. Farber," she heard him say. "I'm in college. I'm studying biology."

Anna bent down to study the jewelry display beside the elevator. She cracked her gum.

"I'm working here for the summer," the bellboy added.

They rode the elevator to the fifth floor.

"You have a nice room," he added, opening the door.

They actually had two rooms, joined by a bathroom, Della noted.

"Well, I'll be going," he said, looking at Anna again.

"Here, son," her father said, giving him a bill.

"Thank you, Mr. Farber. My name is Jack," he said. "Thank you," he repeated, exiting.

"A nice boy," said her mother. "Ohh," she sighed, sitting on the bed, "we're here."

"I'm going swimming" her sister announced.

"No, you're not," her mother said. "You'll catch a cold. You're not used to the weather. What are you doing?" she asked but Anna had already unfastened her suitcase and pulled out her bathing suit.

"Let her go," her father said as he examined the ceiling ducts.

At dinner, Deborah fought with her parents.

They complained about her choices though she ate everything that they served.

"You make me want to barf," Anna told her.

Deborah spilled soda on her dress, ate the whipped cream desserts and rushed out before her parents could say anything.

She went to her room and read.

Soon, she made her way down to the hotel's nightclub. Its entrance was festooned with rows of blinking electric lights. The room was filled with women in low cut sheath dresses and men in boxy suits seated in waves of red leather booths.

The tuxedoed master of ceremony was excitedly waiving his arms.

Someone asked her who she was and led her to her parents' table.

"Where's Anna?" Deborah whispered.

"What?" her mother asked, "I can't hear you."

The orchestra played a loud march.

"Where did Anna go?"

"She went for a walk."

With whom, Deborah wanted to ask, but she remained silent.

It was game night. Up on the stage, guests participated in charades, musical chairs and spelling bees, interrupted by jokes and songs led by the activities director.

"Let's go limbo!" he cried.

People wiggled under a pink bar, repeatedly trekking around the pole to try again after it was lowered. One woman tried to slide under the bar but her prominent breasts made it impossible.

Everyone roared.

The master of ceremonies asked her if she needed any help.

She nodded.

He placed the microphone under his arm and put both hands on her breasts and pushed.

People became incoherent with laughter.

The woman shook her head.

He tried again, straddling her.

She raised a finger.

He stepped back.

She reached inside her dress and pulled out one, then another, tan colored object and threw them towards the back of the stage. They bounced and rolled, coming to rest against the velvet curtain.

People were crying with joy.

The woman jiggled under the bar, accompanied by applause.

Deborah was afraid to glance at her parents.

She exited the nightclub, went to her room and crawled into bed,

The next day she woke early. She could see the sun shining through the horizontal blinds. Anna was curled up in the next bed her hair arranged in a watery looking veil around her head. She smiled as she slept. Deborah dressed and went to the dining room. Few people were present. She ate three or four buttered rolls and several eggs before her parents came down and then ate again.

"What are you going to do today?' her mother asked. "Did you send postcards to your Aunt Edith and Aunt Lilly?"

"No," Deborah said.

"I want you to go right to the desk and ask for postcards and write to them."

"No," Deborah said, even though she liked to write. Everyone said that she had the best handwriting. Anna would even ask her to write her reports until she demanded that their father buy a portable electric typewriter which she refused to share.

"Sophomores have a lot of work!" Anna wailed.

Deborah called it a "bribewriter" and used it whenever Anna was gone.

"Listen to your mother!" her father said.

She walked over to the hotel reception desk. She was a much better daughter than Anns, she thought. It was a wonder that her parents didn't notice it.

The fair haired boy stood at the elevator. "Hi," he said.

"Hi, yourself," Deborah said. "What time is it?" He raised his metal banded wristwatch.

"Ten."

"What are you doing?"

"I'm going swimming. You going?" he asked

"Sure," Deborah replied.

He left.

He's friendly, Deborah thought.

Anna walked out of the elevator.

"Well, well, well. Deborah's got herself a boyfriend," she sang.

"Drop dead," Deborah said, yet pleased.

"What's his name?"

"I don't know," Deborah said, as a bellboy came up to them.

"I'm off again at nine," he said, holding his hands behind his back.

"Hi," Deborah ventured.

"Oh, hi." he answered.

"Really," Anna said, examining the ends of her hair. She was wearing new shorts that revealed her long legs and a shirt that bared her midriff.

"Can I see you?" he asked.

"May-eh-be," Anna said as she strolled off.

The bellboy followed her.

Deborah bit her tongue and wondered what she had said wrong this time.

She jumped in the pool.

The burning green water swallowed her.

She wore a mask and snorkel and floated face down for a long time.

She saw her parents arrive and take possession of slatted chairs and grease each other with suntan lotion.

She pretended to be dead.

She wondered if they would notice.

"Don't you think that it's time that you came out?" she heard her mother call.

She dove to the bottom of the pool and came up and dove again. She felt something grab her ankles and whirled around.

It was the boy. He chased her around the bottom of the pool. She kicked him in his face.

"I'm sorry," she said as they surfaced.

He looked at her as they clung to the side of the pool.

"What's your name?" he asked.

"Deborah Farber. What's yours?"

"Stephen Elephant."

"What kind of name is Elephant?"

"Russian," he said.

"Wow," she said.

"I play the violin in the All-City Orchestra."

"I like violins," she found herself saying, even though she had never heard anyone play a violin.

A waitress came around with a tray of food.

They ate small hot dogs rolled in dough and talked about school.

"Do you want to go to the dance?"

"Sure," she said, "What dance?"

"There's going to be a dance on the boat dock at nine o'clock."

"Okay. See you later."

She returned to her room but found that she couldn't read.

Strands of Anna's hair covered he bathroom sink. Her make-up bag toppled against the faucets, spilling its contents. Della played with the colors until Anna came in and grabbed the bag. They scratched each other but it was Anna who won, having drawn blood. Repentant and threatened byDeborah's declaration that she would tell their mother, Anna agreed to set Deborah's hair.

Deborah sat on the edge of the bathtub as Anna twirled and pinned her short curls, admiring her skill.

"You sure that it'll come out?" Deborah asked.

"Sit still."

"Ouch!" screamed Deborah

"You want it to be good?"

"Not so tight!"

Finally, it was done and Deborah looked at herself in the mirror.

Her round face was surrounded by a metal halo.

"I like it," she said.

"Do you want me to do your make-up?" Anna asked, proudly.

"What are you going to do?"

Anna forced her down on the bed and hovered over her eyes with tweezers.

"Don't move," she said, descending.

She began to tug at Deborah's eyebrow.

Tears formed in her eyes as Anna worked.

She stared at the ceiling and tried not to think of the pain.

Anna wiped her brows with a cotton ball dipped in witch hazel.

"Enough!" shouted Deborah.

Anna handed her a mirror

Where there had once been once wide straight brows, were a thinned pair of arches.

"Wait, I'm not finished," Anna said. She reached into her bag and lay tubes, brushes and cakes across the bed. She smeared green cream on Deborah's eyelids, lined her eyes with black and colored her lashes with blue.

"It brings out your eyes," Deborah heard her say.

She found her face unrecognizable. She looked older, sarcastic, sophisticated.

"Not bad," she said.

They began to dress for dinner.

Anna wore a white dress with a thick ribbon belt that emphasized her narrow waist. Deborah wore a similar dress, several sizes larger. They both wore heels. Deborah tried to walk. Her ankles turned in, then out.

At dinner, her mother said nothing about her new look.

Afterwards, Anna sat in the lobby with three young men, guests of the hotel.

She let one offer her a stick of gum, another tell her of the supposed homosexuality of another. The third pretended to shoot a kiss in her direction.

Deborah walked the grounds of the hotel. She kicked the gravel with her pointed shoes and waited for nine o'clock.

Shrubbery in the center of the sloping lawn was sculpted into the name of the hotel.

The driveway was bordered with colored flowers.

She bent down and fingered their soft petals and looked up at the dark trees at the end of the driveway. She walked to the edge of the road and startled by the headlights of an approaching automobile turned and retraced her steps.

She remembered that once in the bungalow colony she and Anna had gone deep into the woods and until they found a grove of wild berries. They filled their tin pails as they sang popular songs.

They had almost gotten lost, but they hadn't. Anna had almost been stung by a bee, but it had missed. They held hands as they returned to the bungalow. They gave the berries to their aunt and watched as she made an enormous pie. Everyone said that it had been the most delicious pie that they had ever eaten. Her mother hadn't been too angry that they had gone off without telling her. Her father arrived from the city and gave them identical dolls.

It had been a long time ago.

Deborah walked towards the fluorescent lights of the hotel.

She made her way to the boathouse.

People had paired off, dancing and talking.

She looked for Anna but could not find her.

Suddenly, Stephen came up behind her and put his arm around her shoulder.

"Hi," he said.

"Hi," she said.

"You want to dance?"

She wanted to refuse. She did not know how to dance but she soon found that he did not know how to, either. They held on to each other and swayed.

The music changed.

He kissed her cheek.

She drew away.

"I want something to drink," she said.

He brought two cups of soda. "I'm playing for the Mayor in September," he said,

"Really?" she said.

"Yes, I'm the first violinist. Will you come to listen to me after the summer?"

She didn't answer.

He put his drink down and asked her to dance.

The music was slow, so slow, she wondered if it was meant for dancing.

The singer sang of the coincidence both of them loving each other.

Stephen tried to dance off into the shadows.

Deborah resisted.

He tried to kiss her lips.

Deborah turned her head.

They rested in the light.

"My mother says I have to practice two hours every day but I don't care because I'm good," he said.

Another song began and Stephen shoved her into the darkness. She broke loose and tottered off the boat dock in her wobbly heels.

"What's the matter?" she heard him ask.

She walked the back paths to the hotel, removing her shoes, even though she knew that if she tore her stockings, her mother would be angry. She heard a rustling sound. A girl emerged from the woods. Her dress was covered with twigs and mud. Her hair hung wet and disarrayed and her mouth was strangely red and down turned.

"Anna?

She walked up and put her arms around Deborah's stout shoulders. Deborah wasn't sure if she was crying. She slipped an arm around her waist and together they went to their room, unseen, shut the light and tried to sleep.

THE FRAU

I heard a tap at the door.

I slid the metal lid covering the keyhole upwards and looked out.

It was Mrs. Fogel, our neighbor.

I opened the lock.

Mrs. Fogel always dressed in dark, close-fitting dresses. She wore shoes made of expensive Italian leather. Her hair was piled atop her head. A small gold pin sat on her shoulder.

Her manner was tentative.

She turned around. "Please?" she asked, looking coquettishly over her shoulder at me.

Her accent was unlike those of my Polish and Romanian parents. Her clipped tones had a rhythmic Hungarian cadence.

I had always noticed the other-worldly manners of Mrs. Fogel and her husband.

He was courtly. She was charming.

"*Gelibte*! *Teier*!" they called each other.

"*Bitte*!" they said repeatedly.

He wore well made suits. His hair was brushed back from his crown. I had heard that he worked in "insurance" an uncommon profession among the post-Holocaust tailors and entrepreneurs I knew.

They had no children, also an oddity. Survivors commonly sought to reproduce after the war, whether they had a parental nature or not.

Our apartment building was filled with children. My cousins and I and our families occupied five separate units.

But Mrs. Fogel and her husband had their rooms to themselves.

"Please," she asked, again.

The back of her dress was open, the zipper undone.

"Of course," I said, fastening the closure.

"*Danke schoen*," she said, bending slightly.

"Why does she continue to speak German?" I thought to myself. German was the language that had herded my grandparents onto the ramps of Auschwitz and into the gas chambers to their deaths.

"You are welcome," I responded.

She walked away, down the hall towards her apartment.

"Where could she be going all dressed up in the middle of the day?" I wondered.

I noticed a slight hump marring her once regal postures. Her hair, dyed a chestnut brown, seemed static and fixed in place by sprays and pins.

"Mom," I told my mother later that night, "Mrs. Fogel was here today. She asked me to close her dress."

"Poor woman," my mother said.

"What do you mean?"

My mother busied herself peeling a potato.

"What are you making?" I asked

"A meat loaf."

"What did you mean 'poor woman'"?

She lowered her voice.

"Cancer. She has breast cancer."

"Oh."

"When are you going back to college?" she asked.

"Next Tuesday."

I picked a cucumber slice out of the salad she had prepared.

"When is Dad coming home?"

"He's on his way."

"I have some reading to do."

"So, go do it."

"How come Mrs. Fogel never had any children?"

My mother looked up.

"Why would you ask such a thing?"

"I don't know. I was just wondering. They seem so devoted to each other."

"He's a good man."

"Did you know them before you came to America?"

She shook her head.

"Were they in camp?"

"I don't know."

"Were they married before the war?"

My mother shrugged her shoulders.

I sat down at the kitchen table.

She looked at me.

"What do you think of Leah's boyfriend?" I asked.

"He's a good catch. He's in medical school."

"Oh, mom. Money isn't everything."

"Your sister likes rich things."

"They are going out Saturday night."

"Where?"

"His aunt. She's having a birthday party. They sure spend a lot of time together."

"First, your sister, then you."

"Ma!"

"First, your sister."

I stood up, enraged.

"There's more to life than getting married!"

She smiled.

"You know what your father's mother used to say? '*Ah kiss und ah glet bleibt nist kan flek.*'"

"What?"

"You understand."

"No, I don't."

"A boy. He just leaves. A girl has to be smart."

"Ugh."

"She said it to her daughters, daddy's sisters."

"Please."

"I know what I am talking about."

"What about Mrs. Fogel? Is she going to be all right?"

"It's in God's hands."

"She seems lonely. I wonder why she never had any children."

"After the war, '*zi ot zich gekalya gemakht.*"

My mother's words numbed me.

She had "ruined" herself, my mother said.

Pregnant, maybe in dire straits, maybe unwilling to bear life so soon after so many had lost theirs, maybe reluctant to share her life with anyone other than her husband, she had had an abortion. Afterwards, she was unable to have children.

We moved away from the apartment house the next year, losing contact with Mrs. Fogel and our other neighbors.

Later, I heard that Mrs. Fogel died and that her dignified, attentive and loving husband had remarried.

WHITE MAN, FAT MAN

He tore the page from the desk calendar. It was no longer October twenty-fourth. His pale fingers crumpled the paper into a ball. He switched on the overhead lamp. A circled red "X" was printed on the new date.

"Mr. Burke!"

He looked up. "What?"

Gladys stood beside him her heavy speckled arms folded across her chest. She cracked her chewing gum. "I have been standing here for five minutes. Are you asleep? Joy, tell him how long I been standing here."

Joy shut the file cabinet and laughed, her eyes crinkling in her face. "I don't know." She lowered herself into a swivel chair and shook her head.

Gladys sighed. "Here are the checks for Mr. Stone to sign. God only knows," she muttered "what he does behind that desk."

He raised his blotter and withdrew a pamphlet titled Basic "Nutrition Requirements" He examined the contents as he munched a doughnut.

"Mr. Burke! Your PHONE IS RINGING!" Gladys sang above the clatter of typewriters.

"Where?" he asked.

"On your DESK," she responded. "Looks like Christmas is early this year, Joy. Santa brought us a real fruitcake."

He picked up the receiver. "Yes, sir," he said. "Right away, Mr. Stone. I'll be right in." He gathered the checks. Refolding the pamphlet, he placed it under a calculator. He leaned forward as he walked past the office machines and personnel.

"Wowee," Gladys cried. "What a loser! Is he or is he not a case? Tell me."

He ground his heels into the orange carpet. "Mr. Stone, I'm leaving."

Mr. Stone peered over the rims of his glasses. "But Burke, Major, you're my Accounts Payable. What's the matter? Haven't we treated you nice?"

"I'm leaving. Sir."

"But why, Major?"

"I'm leaving, today, Mr. Stone. Sir."

Mr. Stone put his party on hold and his cigar in his ashtray. Leaning back in his leather chair, he hooked his thumbs in his vest pockets. "Leaving? No. You're not leaving, no. You, Burke, are not leaving. YOU'RE GETTING KICKED OUT. YOU'RE FIRED! GET OUT! GET OUT!"

Returning to his desk, Major taped a list of departmental operating instructions onto the calendar and then left the office.

Children ran back and forth along the streets, fighting playing, shouting. He wondered why they were not in school. All children should be in school, he thought. He entered a supermarket. Its windows were boarded and bricked, its doors reinforced with steel bars. "Love" a voice sang over the store intercom "Is a Many Splendored Thing". He rolled a cart down the aisle. Berry, apple, cherry. He gathered the pies in his arms. He picked up a carton of ice-cream.

"Mister! Would yuh look out for crissakes?"

Major disentangled his cart and pushed on. Rolls. Raisins. Crackers. Cookies.

He handed the cashier money.

The iridescent traveling clock on the coffee table ticked rhythmically.

Major lay down on a plastic covered sofa beneath a set of watercolor portraits of ballerinas. He lived in three small rooms in a government housing complex. The buildings were uniformly constructed, down to the alternating pink and green hallways on each floor.

Major's apartment was next to the incinerator. Its proximity would help.
He removed his shoes and placed them in the closet. An empty birdcage was
perched on a stack of magazines beside his bed. The bird had helped him,
too. Each day he had fed it more grain, added supplements to its water, left
treats suspended on its wooden perch. One morning he awoke to find the
bird dead. The glass water cups in the cage glistened. He reached inside the
cage and pushed the swing.

The kettle whistled in the kitchen. He rose and closed the blinds.

He began.

He made an entry in his log under the heading "Week One".

In upright letters linked by crescent strokes, he wrote "Approximate Gain
Over Actual Gain".

He hoped to achieve net profit of five percent on his predicted goal of
five sixteen.

He dusted the apartment daily, mopped the floors weekly. He saw
himself acting in concert with great historical figures. They, like he, had
undertaken difficult tasks and through their extraordinary courage, above
and beyond the call of duty, had been able to surmount huge and numerous
obstacles. He considered himself to be on a journey. He had stocked rations
and had arranged for regular delivery of additional supplies. His task did
have its tests, its rigors, its discipline of six meals per day. But he would face
them one at a time, according to schedule. He recalled the words of the
television minister. "Who are we," he had shouted, "to stand in the way of
the Lord God? We plead and beg for time when it is time to die, for peace
when we cry and pity when we transgress. Who are we to interfere in the
way he rules the earth? He did ask us when he created the cosmos and set
the galaxies spinning. He did not ask us when he rested. How does man
attempt to change the ways of the Lord. Why," he demanded, raising the
arms of his striped robe to the heavens "does man presume, presume to
challenge the word of the Almighty? Because, because man is so
meaningless, is of such infinitesimal value that he does not recognize his
own nothingness." Major would persevere. He would succeed. He had a
plan. He had worked for fifteen years with people who had disliked him. He

had been ignored and surrounded. Here in the apartment, eating most of the day, sleeping most of the night, he was content, at peace.

By the end of the second week, he could feel the changes. His expanding abdomen was joined by softening, spreading hips. His ribs disappeared. His arms felt solid.

By the end of the month his round face was supported by a thick neck and barrel shaped torso. Dimples appeared on the backs of his hands. But he had only gained eighteen pounds. He would try to relax, only think of pleasant things. His book, the man. It has been his most valuable possession. He purchased a cover to protect it. His mother had thrown it away. She said it had been an accident. He didn't really believe her. It had been an encyclopedia of world records. One entry especially impressed him. It read "Isaiah Octavius McKinley of Macon, Georgia, while working in a circus, gained the most amount of weight in the shortest amount of time, surpassing three hundred and twenty-five pounds in six months. McKinley was the star of the Fat Man exhibit and one season, as a promotional stunt, had been fed superhuman amounts of food. Towards the end of his life, he ceased performing. He was no longer mobile. His skin had lost its elasticity. When he died, they were forced to cut open the top of his trailer and lift him out with a crane." Major could visualize the scene. Suspended in mid-air, gently lowered to the ground, grieved for by the acrobats, midgets and clowns. They wept, acknowledging the passing of one of the best. He was unique.

ii

He wondered where the snow had gone. The day before, sheets of snow had fallen from the gray November sky. He reread his old magazines and listened to his seventy-eights. How long would he remain undiscovered if he fell ill? What if someone became suspicious or he was seen on a midnight foray to the mailbox? He would let them in if they tried to enter and pretend that their intrusion was meaningless. He would invite them to stay. He would not be too gregarious. He would be busy, active in some activity, cooperate but not volunteer.

Time was his enemy. He followed the calendar faithfully. His body grew. His clothes no longer fit. He roamed the rooms in a sheet, wrapped toga-like around his body. His eyes became slits in his face, his hair matted around his ears. When he positioned himself on the sofa his belly reached over his thighs. He could not cross his legs. He stopped cleaning the apartment, the exertion weakened him. December and January passed. The pages of the log were half filled.

The apartment walls were thin. Major could hear crying children and violent arguments. On Lincoln's birthday, while playing Danny Kaye's recording of "Molly Malone", he heard six shots. From his window, Major watched a man being led to a squad car. He swung at an officer and caught him on the jaw with his handcuffs.

Sitting in his kitchen, he could listen to the pneumatic sounds of the elevator and the conversations of arriving and departing people.

One day, while he was treating a nosebleed, the doorbell rang.

Once. Twice. Three times.

Major remained still.

"Yoo-hoo, Mr. Burke!"

It was Mrs Rossi. She was dangerous. She could notify someone. Why was she coming to his apartment? The few times they had met she would chatter, standing in her tent-like housedress and furry slippers, about how "they" were all over the neighborhood. One of them had even tried to call up her Cecilia. You could tell. They never learned to talk like normal people. It was also a matter of biology. You had to stop feeding them with giant welfare checks. In China they knew enough to leave defective babies to die on a hill in the country. Major would say he was expecting a telephone call to get away. Sometimes, she didn't understand him. She was somewhat deaf. He would wave to her as he backed down the hall as she continued to talk.

He heard a rustle of paper, a tearing of tape.

He heard the clank of a chain, then a lock.

He waited.

Finally, he walked to his door and opened it.

A blue lined sheet fluttered with the motion.

He grabbed it and pushed the door shut.

"Neighbor. There has been a great deal of garbage around the incinerator lately. It is dangerous to our health! Please place your things in the chute. Don't leave your garbage around for everyone to vomit. Please join in. There are ways and means to find you if you think you are getting away with it. Very Sincerely Yours, Fourth Floor Cleanliness. Mrs. Virginia Rossi."

How could she accuse him? It was anyone but him. It was that young dancer down the hall. All he did was play loud music and have parties and never go to work.

Major turned on the radio.

"A Pretty Girl Is Like a Melody," a man crooned.

"March 28, the world premiere of 'Where Giants Stood', a revolutionary new feature film about the destruction of the dinosaurs. Starring Awa Usilin and Gars Telbrecht. Directed by the award winning Icelandic director, Nimsey Edjqyck. Now at your local --"

He unplugged the radio.

It would be very cold that evening. There was great risk. The rent was due and Meyer would have to ride the elevator before dawn to the mail drop in the windy first floor vestibule. His robe was stained with sweat and grease of countless fried meals. His protuberant lips rested on a wiry brown beard. He could feel his cheeks touch the top of his eye sockets. He felt detached from his body, as if he could abandon it at will.

iii

"Gay Divorcee" with Ginger Rogers and Fred Astaire was listed for four-thirty. It was one of his favorites. Dozens of people dressed in black and white changed partners and costumes with each new movement.

Major heard a siren

A crowd was gathered in the courtyard.

"Maaa! Throw me down some money!" a child cried. "I want to go to the candy store!"

Women in hair curlers, boys in mud streaked football jerseys and girls hugging dolls stood around a concrete bench. Stretcher bearers divided the group.

Major could see the figure of a man, knees drawn to his chest, hands pressed against his abdomen as he rolled from side to side. The attendants grasped his ankles and his wrists and lowered him onto the canvas.

He entered the kitchen and ate a pastry. He licked the chocolate from his fingers and then ate another. The sight of the man moved him. He took a roll out of the breadbox. He had been helpless. Major wondered, as he peeled a banana, at his own success. Nothing came between him and his actions, no second thoughts. He finished a cream pie and laughed in high pitched chuckles as he tore open a bag of marshmallows. Stabbing several with a serving fork, he roasted them over the gas burner. As their white surface blackened, they emitted a brown flame. Reheated bacon fat began to sizzle in the caked trays on the range. Majr supported his elbow with his palm and began to sing, waving the utensil in time to the beat.

"We Were Sailing Along Down Moonlight Bay. We could hear the voices singing, they seemed to say." He bit into the marshmallows and dropped them with a shout. Ice in his mouth, he ambled into the bathroom. He searched among suppositories and band-aids until he found a tube of ointment. His finger rested on his bottom lip. He would miss the movie if he didn't hurry.

A board creaked.

Major turned off the faucet.

The linoleum squeaked.

"Put up you hands!" a man hissed, pointing a pistol at Major.

His legs were bent at the knees. His eyes shone in his wide, dark face.

"You move now!"

The movie must have started, Major thought. He hoped that it was just a commercial.

The man ran a hand through his oily hair. A jagged cut glistened beneath his open shirt.

"Do you want some help?" Major asked.

The man gestured."Out!"

"Are you sure?"

"Get out!"

Major faced the door frame and edged out. As he made his way, leaning on one limb, then the other, his stomach heaved and his legs vibrated. Pushing aside an empty cereal carton on the floor, he entered the living room.

"Now, look, mom, you doan move or I gonna hafto keel you. Unnerstan?"

Major nodded.

"Christos," the man muttered. "Look, you gotta give me you money, now. No funny bizness. I not afraid to keel you. Unnerstan?"

"Yes. But I have no money," Major said.

"You doan unnerstan! I doan keer if you get keeled, mon. I doan keer. Han over the money. Now!" The man put the gun to Major's temple.

"Yes. I understand. But I have no--."

The man cocked the trigger. "Hey Fat Man. You wanna die?"

He pressed the muzzle into Major's skull. "You see the man inna fron? You gonna catch his cole. From me."

Major faced the man.

How to end this? There was nothing of value in the apartment. He could take the appliances. They had only been stamp redemptions. And the magazines and three suits. There were some supplies in the bedroom and his seventy-eights. The man removed a knife from his pointed toe ankle boot. Their heels were worn. One boot had a hole beside the big toe. He held the knife in the air.

"You crazy sonafabitch!" he cried.

The knife descended. It was double edged and had an ivory handle.

Somewhere around his navel, Major estimated, the blade entered his body.

Had the ancients felt this way? He was all of them. He was God. But why had his hand not been stayed? He certainly must have known what would happen. He is all knowing. There must be a plan here somewhere.

To market, to market, to buy a new kid.

Home again, home again.

Did it. He did.

iv

"Watch the monitor for arrest. It's not uncommon for cardiacs to repeat while in the hospital."

"But Nurse Phillips. I'm just a first year student. I've never--."

"That's all right. He's almost gone anyway. Have you ever seen anyone so big?"

"Uh-uh!"

"It's enough to make you give up dessert."

THE GREEK

His narrow rib cage, emphasized by his bustier reminded her of a twelve
year old girl's.

When he wasn't wearing a costume (the green velvet gown was his
favorite) he wore jeans and a shirt.

But it was the gown that made him come alive.

Its hem swept along the sodden streets of the city where they attended
college.

The sun rarely emerged in the winter months.

The roads seemed filled with smells of sulfur and wet wool.

When it snowed, it snowed for hours, days. The white mass rose higher
and higher, covering the cars and reaching the second stories of the old
houses. Incongruously (for the weather was inhospitable most of the year),
many of the houses had wide porches.

He was Greek.

He came from an immigrant family downstate.

"I bet he doesn't wear those outfits at home", she mused. "His father
would kill him."

She thought that he knew it as well and that it fueled his whirlwind
behavior of exhibitionism and entertainment.

The neighborhood where she was raised was filled strangely dressed men
as well. They wore black belted robes and fur hats. They had long side curls
that swung across their breasts as they walked. When they would see her
coming, they would leave the sidewalk.

At first, she thought, "George is a hero!"

"He has confronted his inner desires", she told herself.

"Quel courage!" (Two years of college French and a summer abroad had equipped her to use the occasional Gallic phrase.)

George was acerbic.

"He's candid! Honest. Tells the truth!"

He twitched.

"He's energetic!"

He was engaged in frenzied activities.

"He's adventuresome!"

Was witty1

He was mean.

Sometimes, she felt that she had had her fill of him but then the motherly, nurturing side of her overcame her and she continued to spend time with him and accompany him to parties.

When George wore the dress and his stubble was at its darkest and his curls, their wildest, she felt as if he were making a bold statement. Slight of build, clearly a man, he dared the world to say something to him, confront him.

They never did.

At home, she rarely opposed her domineering father or tried to communicate with her passive mother. She had long ago ceased seeking their approval. Yet, she knew that she carried them within herself and being with George was a statement of her rebellion and rejection of their conformity.

Then, one day, she decided to change George, to make him like women.

"He's very masculine", she thought. "He just hasn't met the right girl."

She knew that he liked her. Despite the fact that he was rude to her, he kept returning. He had exhausted all his other friends, who eventually left him, including another young man who also wore a dress. He, though, failed to impress her as George had, with his Medusa-like coiffure and swarthy looks. He was just a skinny boy with strangely clumping brown hair and uneven features.

One day, George brought over a box of cupcakes.

She was surprised. He rarely gave her a gift.

They talked or rather, she talked as he spit out short sentences and his shoulders rose and fell electrically.

It was a gray, somber day, yet somehow within her nondescript bedroom, it was cozy. She burned an almond scented candle and sat cross legged on her chenille bedspread.

George smoked a cigarette.

He rose and went to her bookshelf and withdrew a book.

In a soft, calm voice, he read a poem.

Suddenly, he looked as handsome as a figure in a classic sculpture. His beautiful profile, his gallant head, bent over the book. His long, sensitive fingers followed the text.

She lay back on her bed.

He reached out and touched her hair strewn across the pillows.

Leaning over, he kissed her lips.

She felt as if she were being bussed by a child.

She moved over, as if to make room for him.

Neither spoke.

He lay alongside her.

Her legs extended past his.

He turned to her.

He kissed her again, this time, with greater force.

She knew that if she spoke, he would leave.

She placed her hands between his legs.

He shuddered.

His kisses were harder and harder.

She fumbled with his zipper.

He placed his hands on her breast, her hips, exploring her body, memorizing her anatomy.

She touched his warm, flush organ. She heard him groan.

Suddenly, they heard a door slam.

The others had returned.

He rose, quickly fastening his pants.

She sat up.

"We're going to the club tonight. If you want to come," he said, over his shoulder, as he danced out of the room.

"Sure," she said to his departing shadow.

She slammed the door and murmured her thanks and something about the weather and how she thought it was a crime more people didn't stop for hitchhikers.

"I'm a sex maniac," the man said, smiling shyly.

She looked at him with interest.

"That's all right," she said, "we all are."

"But I'm giving you a ride, what are you going to give me?" he giggled.

"I'll give you a ride if I ever see you hitching. I hate skiing. You really have to be in top form, physically. I remember when I went skiing they were carrying people off the hill as if there had been a war."

"I need some loving. Hmn. I'm not going to let you forget that. I'm going to make you change your mind."

"Do you have any idea how fast they go? Forty, fifty miler an hour."

"Do you want to stop for coffee?"

She looked at her boot. The snow was beginning to melt and creep in between the seams. She glanced at the side of the road. A neon sign declaring BLAZING TEXAS RED HOTS fired the overcast sky.

"Oh, no," she said good humouredly. "I have to get off soon. Well, what did you think of the game last night?"

"They got some forward."

"He's my brother," she said.

"No kidding!"

"Oh, yeah. We used to play together as kids. Then my dad was killed in the war and we kind of cut it out.

"What war? Where are you going anyhow?"

"You know, the last one, this one. He was a demo...demolition expert and a …wrestling coach. His men were working out in a field one day and hit a mine. He thought it was his and he volunteered for this special assignment everyone knew was suicide. It turns out when they put all the pieces together they discovered it wasn't his after all."

"You mean it wasn't his mine?"

"It wasn't …his men."

"Jeez." He pulled over to allow an ambulance to pass. She unraveled her scarf and sighed.

"Um, he didn't die either. He was shot by his orderly in a poker game."

"You never know," he offered, rejoining the traffic. "You want a piece of gum?"

"Thanks. My mom always warned him he'd die because of cards. That's where they met, my mom and dad, at a card table. She was a professional dealer in Vegas but she could take it or leave it. She left it for my brother and me. She used to call us 'the aces of her eye!'"

"Look, what time do you have to be at the place where you are going?"

"Really soon." She leaned back and rested her elbow against the window. "Terrible weather."

"Are you a lover?" he asked, turning in her direction.

She gathered her bag of books and placed them on her thighs. "Of course," she said brightly, popping a lavender bubble. He gave her a mildly sinister leer.

"How about giving me some loving?" He began to pick up speed.

"I am not," she insisted, raising her head delicately, "a prostitute."

"Oh, no," he sputtered, "I didn't say that, I know that. I just, well, uh, you know I…"

"That's okay," she said and opened a side vent on the dashboard.

They turned onto a main avenue in silence.

"What's that?" he asked, reaching across her abdomen. She moved quickly.

"This?" she demanded, fingering a yellow ticket. "Oh, that's from skiing. We talked about that, remember?"

"Are you from the university?" he asked suddenly.

"I got a volleyball scholarship. You know, the height and all. My family's tall. So was my father until he died. We got the flag that covered his coffin. It was extra big, his coffin. They buried him in Arlington right near the president. Every Sunday thousands of people pass his grave and they are all mourning. Of course not for my dad, but the mood carries over."

"Because if you're from there…" he started, growing angry.

"Where?"

"That place…"

"Virginia?"

"No, the university. Because I'm going to tell you right here what I think of them. They are the worst bunch of sons of bitches I ever seen and if I met one of them on a dark street alone at night I'd run them over right then and there and not think twice about it. They're filthy. I got this buddy who says they run around naked in the apartment below his and they don't care where they do it."

"Even in the road."

"What"

"Yeah, I agree with you. No, I don't go to the university."

"But you said you got a scholarship."

"I did, didn't I? I'm not supposed to tell anyone about that. Don't you go and tell anyone about that. We had a lot of trouble getting it past those, you know, who run the student government. I mean I don't go like they go. I support the president. I worked in his office, even."

"Yeah?"

"I fixed his executive chair. I do carpentry, part time," she said breaking out in a laugh which she turned into a cough. "The weather, bad lungs, hereditary, my mom's family were coal miners."

"We were farmers."

"What did you farm?"

"Cabbage."

"I like cabbage. My dad was Irish."

"You sure talk a lot about your family."

"We were very close." She gazed around the red interior of the vehicle. She glanced at a tackle box in the rear seat. "You fish?" she inquired politely, eyeing the street signs.

"Naw, them's my tools."

"You're a mechanic?"

"No, a butcher."

"Well, she announced, "I'll be getting off soon, next block." She grit her teeth.

"Aw, why can't I change your mind?"

"People are expecting me."

"Who?" he asked, removing one hand from the steering wheel and dropping it to the torn seat cushion.

"My, my. I'm late already."

"Who?" he repeated, moving his hand beside the folds of her coat.

"My driving teacher."

"How come you have to go to him?"

"I… well, today's Sunday." They stopped for a red light. She grasped the door handle.-

"Will you wait a minute!" he protested but she had opened the car door and stepped out into the slush filled intersection. He grasped her scarf and pulled. They stared at each other. She gently unfolded his fingers.

"Thank you," she called as she shut the door and began to walk across the lanes of steaming cars, buttoning every button of her coat and hiding her face in the fabric of her collar.

COMMERCE

They had been in her kitchen for two days, the three of the, smoking and
carrying on. When she gone to bed the first and second nights, they
remained clustered around the rickety table beside the filmed over window.
On the third day she was sent out for cigarettes. As another night fell, she
hoped that someone would suggest taking a ride somewhere but the rapid
conversation continued, pierced only by startling cries or laughter and her
hopes died. She gathered the folds of the dress that she was making and
settled into a corner of the kitchen. Was there time to go for tea before the
store closed, they asked. She clutched the money that one of the men had
given her and ran down the stairs. She wondered, as she walked bareheaded
in the bitter wind, at how they were able to go on. She slowly walked the
aisles in the market. She would surprise them, she decided, left the store and
entered a bakery. She stood and watched her reflection in its mirrored walls
until a saleswoman demanded to know if she could help her. She counted the
correct change for a dozen doughnuts. She strolled back over the hard
broken earth of the unpaved road. She found that they had left the door open
although she had begged them not to. But then she remembered that she had
been the last to leave and that it was she that had left the door ajar.

"Our Japanese lady is back," one of the men exclaimed.

"Have you brought us some goodies?"

"What has she done this time?" asked the woman.

She glowed and joined in the banter for a while but soon found herself
withdrawing. Would they sleep this night? She wanted them all to fall down
and sleep for hours the way they had done the last time. She took the dress
to her room. She pinned the collar, softly singing the words of a ballad she
had seen in a magazine and whose melody she imagined. The facing of the
collar had been badly cut and its ends did not meet. The woman had insisted
on helping. She made tiny darts in the material and discovered it turn into a
ruffle.

"What time is it?" a voice called.

They wanted her. She swung off the bed.

"Come here, the artist will tell us what she thinks."

The older man grasped her wrist and propelled her towards his knee. He smoothed her buttocks as he repeated his request, his fingers tracing the hand sewn flowers on the bank of her kimono.

"I think of death as having something to do with the time that you die. If you die at dusk or at dawn, it's best. But if you die in the night or in the morning, everything is made certain and if you die in the afternoon, you'll never know." She scraped at the caked gum on the plastic tablecloth. The woman touched her head.

"Your hair is so beautiful. Come, I want to fix you up."

They walked beside each other to the bedroom.

"Sit."

She worked silently, her thin fingers twisting and pulling.

"I can't see your eyes. Look up"

The girl lifted her solemn face. She felt herself unevenly seated on the wooden chair. She let her eyes droop and her lower jaw lie limp and her lips suspend in a pout. Her arms circled her ribs and she massaged their blunt ripples. The woman said that she was done.

"Sayonara!" the men said, when she returned.

"I want to take pictures," one announced. He unsnapped the leather case of his camera and removed the silver and blue felt lens cover and blew on it. He held a floodlight and shouted directions from behind the painful brightness as they posed in changing patterns.

"Oh, enough." the woman said, resting against the porcelain sink.

She returned to her room and danced and stretched and wept as she touched the dusty floor with her forehead. She traced the divisions of the floorboards in the darkness. The sounds echoed. She was confident that it must soon be over. One more day. They would leave quickly. It was always over by then and they would leave.

"And here he is!" she heard them cry.

She grasped the material of her robe and raced into the kitchen.

"What have you got there, my boy?"

"Come on, come on."

"I must see."

He was worn. Grey half-moons underlined his eyes. He sniffed and glanced around the room.

"It was cold out there, yessir, it was."

She moved to the window as they surrounded him.

"C'mon!" shrieked the woman as they laughed.

"How was my old lady while I was gone?" he asked.

"Look, man."

"I'm fine."

"It's in the car, wrapped and ready to go," he said, handing them the keys.

They grabbed their coats and hugged him and left. He turned and walked out of the room. She followed him. He threw himself on the bed. She sat beside him. She unbuttoned his jacket and flannel shirt and ran her fingers across his chest with increasing pressure.

"Aren't you curious about what happened?" he asked.

She unfastened his heavy belt.

"Yes, I am."

"I was arrested and I got off, could only get off by turning them in."

He picked at am upper tooth.

"I think I have a cavity. What do you think of that?" he asked.

"Nothing," she said, rising. She unlaced his boots and set them down. He removed the rest of his clothing and she undid the sash of her robe.

"Got to get it looked at," he yawned, turning off the lamp and rolling over.

She slipped beneath the covers and until the sun ended their play, followed the car headlights beaming, moving, darkening and reappearing above her wall mounted drawings and clay figures.

FISHING IN THE INTERCOASTAL

The sea was green. An hour or so earlier, it had been steel gray. Now, like some animated blanket, the verdant water cover spread towards their eighteen- foot motorboat.

She had never been on the sea before, having been born and raised in a large, noisy city.

The silence and empty space of the horizon were unsettling.

The boat was made of fiberglass. Discarded beer cans rolled on its bottom. The turquoise vinyl seats were worn and cracked, the plastic windshield dull.

They had borrowed the boat for the day.

She held her fishing pole lamely in her hand, reluctant to reel in the line, lest she discover that she had no bait and would have to reach into the bucket and pinion another squirrelly, tomato-seed eyed shrimp.

The boat had no radio, no flares and no water.

Feelings of restlessness swelled her body.

"What am I doing here?" she thought.

She would have liked to have stayed back in the apartment and work the crossword puzzle in the out of town newspaper. The local paper published announcements of picnics, bible meetings and the county fair.

"I can't live in a place that has no sidewalks," she had cried.

But he asked her to stay. It was his hometown.

She tried to concentrate on the novelty of her surroundings.

Floating beds of seaweed clumped around the hull. A flying fish broke the surface, a sea turtle passed by.

"We're trolling," he said, as the boat began to run in a wide circle.

"Trolling," she thought, "what a funny word." She felt dizzy and hot. It reminded her of when she had been a child and had spun and danced in purposeless orbits until she had collapsed, breathless, with near loss of consciousness.

She stared as he cast his line.

"Feel anything?" he asked.

"No," she said.

When they had first come into the open sea this day after days in the intercoastal waterway, she had announced, as she had the other days, "Okay, throw out the anchor!"

The bottom, he explained, was hundreds of feet beneath them. The chain securing the anchor was thirty feet long.

"Oh," she responded.

"A storm's coming," he said.

She looked up. The sun was shining overhead.

"Over there," he said, pointing to the far south where clouds had gathered. "It'll be here in twenty minutes," he said. "We'd better head in."

He reeled in his line and set his rod in the rod well and reached for her rod and did the same.

She sat alongside him and watched him, his wavy dark hair spilling over his visor, shading his black eyes. When she had first met him she had thought him exotic, some wayfarer or sailor from a far off port. He regaled her with stories of surfing and shark bites, fishing and tropical summers. They had gone off together. It seemed as if she had found a new world.

He turned the key in the ignition. The small red lighthouse affixed to

the key chain jingled as the engine sputtered and died. He strode to the rear
of the boat and knelt beside the engine, turning knobs and pulling handles.
Suddenly, he stood up and leaned over the side of the boat, retching.

"What's the matter?" she asked.

"Gasoline fumes," he said gasping. "Can you drive the boat?"

"No. I mean, I've never driven one before. If you can show me how," she
said as he slumped on the floor of the boat.

A cool breeze passed over her as the sun disappeared behind a cloud.

"It doesn't matter. I don't think it'll start."

"What'll we do?" she asked.

 "Wait."

She looked around. The waves lapped the sides of the boat. The shrimp
darted in the bucket, their transparent bodies and whiskered antennae
colliding aimlessly against each other. She sighed. She stared at the
ocean, cupped her hand and let the water run over it. The drying salt
stiffened her fingers. Following him south had been an adventure. Now, they
were alone on the shifting sea.

Suddenly, heavy driving rain filled the air. The boat began to fill with
water. He threw a life jacket in her direction. It smelled of mildew. He drew
close and helped her into it. It was very tight, fit for a large child. She picked
up the bucket and, throwing the shrimp overboard, began to bail.

"This is where I end my days," she thought.

She was surprised to find herself calm. She wondered what her family up
north was doing. She regretted that they hadn't caught anything. After days
of throwing croakers and parrot fish back into the intercoastal, she had
hoped for a large grouper. She watched him, bent over the engine and
smiled. Their clothes were pressed to their bodies by the pelting rain.

Abruptly, the motor started and he quickly moved to head the boat to shore. The torn seat pricked the back of her leg as they hit the waves with increasing speed.

"He said I should be conducting services in a pig sty," the aging *gabbai* said.

At first I thought the statement shocking.

After all, there's nothing worse than calling a Jew a "pig".

But, as I watched him, framed by the rustling palm fronds visible through the window, dispassionately recite an incident that had taken place earlier in the week, I nearly laughed.

"That's not very nice," I said.

"That's not all," he continued. "He chased Milton into the parking lot and threatened him. He said that he mispronounced Resnick's Hebrew name when he gave him an *aliya*."

Now, I was laughing.

Inwardly, of course.

Grandfathers, battling in the sub-tropical sun, I thought.

"That's terrible," I responded. "They could get heart attacks."

"I went in another door," he offered. "I didn't want to run into him."

I knew the man of whom he spoke. Lemelman, the paint manufacturer. He was, as they say, high strung. "From narrow lips," my mother used to say, "one should flee." There were rumors about him. I, myself, had had the misfortune to be the target of one of his outbursts. One Sabbath, as he marched around the synagogue, carrying the sacred *sefer torah* scrolls, covered in maroon velvet and decorated with gold embroidered crowns and lions, he passed me, solemnly standing, filled with spiritual peace, when, from under his *tallis*, draped piously on his head, he hissed, "There's that God damned Abraham Schuster. Why is your husband talking to him?"

I was startled out of my reverie, plucked from my sojourn with Joseph and his brothers in the land of Goshen where they had settled seeking isolation from Egypt's decadence, idolatry, excess and lack of a personal relationship with God.

"What have I got to do with whom he speaks?" I whispered. I immediately regretted my response. I should have said was "It is improper to use such words in *schul.*"

"Look at him," he spat.

I was unsure if he was referring to my husband, with whom I had had my own disputes or Schuster, who parenthetically was worthy of the worst invectives.

I refused to turn around and gaze at the direction in which Lemelman was staring.

"I don't understand how grown men could act like this," I responded to the *gabbai,* "and they say women are emotional."

He nodded. He appeared to wish to share more information but I didn't encourage him. I was mindful of the restriction against gossip. People said that Lemelman was in the Mafia, but I would not repeat it. After all, it was *loshen hora.*

"What's the matter with your husband?" another man asked as I walked over to the *kiddish* table to spoon some tuna fish salad on a paper plate for my two-year old daughter.

I thought.

"He was here, you know. He left. His back."

"His back?"

"Yes, it's serious. He was in the hospital."

I omitted the fact that he had been hospitalized several months ago.

The man nodded.

"He had a shot of cortisone. But we think he'll get better. They recommended that he start physical therapy. He'll be getting better," I assured him, guiltily.

Yes, his back hurt but his real problem was that he was unable to enter Goshen, the Sinai camp, Beersheba or any other land of our forefathers.

It was his manner.

He had been a surfer.

The beach had been his *heder.* His surfboard was his *schulan aruch.* He had spent half his life sunburned and wet. He loved ketchup and sugary cola drinks and ate pies piled high with pasty looking, artificial whipped cream.

He drove a boat and fished.

In the ocean.

My parents had refused to believe that he was a Jew even after I showed them his bar mitzvah photographs.

"Bar mitzvah pictures can be faked," my mother responded.

I was incredulous.

How could bar mitzvah pictures be faked?

I didn't know it then, but my mother was a prophet.

"Hopefully, he'll be back next week," I offered.

"Do you know where the rabbi is?" someone asked.

"No. Probably on vacation," I said.

"It's not the same when he's not here," she commented, between bites of *cholent.*

"Ladies and Gentlemen."

The *gabbai* stood up.

"I'm not going to ask for a show of hands but I want a *minyun* tomorrow morning, not a minynette. Please be here. You'll be out in forty-five minutes."

He sat down.

"He should say 'Gentlemen', a woman announced. "Ladies don't count."

I sighed.

No sermon.

No comments on the completion of the Book of Leviticus.

Earlier, the reader had chanted a list of rules concerning agriculture but like all rules of the torah were also aimed at conditioning human behavior, uplifting us from a self-directedness to a consciousness of natural resources, the distinction between work and servitude and recognition of one's unique role in communal life. Fields were to lie fallow after seven years. Land returned to its owners. The Jubilee year. As was the custom, upon finishing one of the five Books of Moses, we had all stood and shouted "*Chazek! Chazek! Venischazeik!*" confirming ourselves to "Be Strong! Be Strong! And may we grow in strength!"

"You know." I said to the Israeli artist. "I finally understand one of my father's expressions. He used to say, '*Vie sieben, vie siebitsk*' I used to think he didn't like children, saying that as you are at seven you will be at seventy but today's torah portion says that many things in Jewish life are measured in terms of seven because that's how long it took God to create the world. Including *Shabbos*, of course."

He looked at me blankly.

"I mean no phrase in Jewish life is used idly. It was a reference to Genesis."

He smiled.

"Do you get any inspiration from biblical sources?"

"Not really."

"Oh."

He drank from his Styrofoam cup.

"Have you ever read Isaac Bashevis Singer?"

"I don't like to read."

"Oh."

"Morris," I said to the estate jeweler, a Holocaust survivor from a hamlet near my mother's. "Did the Jews in Europe work the land in the seventh year?"

"No," he said, reaching for a piece of *bobka.*

"Would you like some tuna fish?" I asked.

"I don't eat that *chazerai*"

"Well, if they didn't work the fields, what did they do? They didn't just sit around for a year."

"No, of course not," he said. "They worked."

"Maybe they became jewelers."

He smiled.

"Could be," he said, finishing the cake.

My daughter refused to eat the tuna fish.

"Too hot," she said.

Hot? Hot tuna fish?

I looked in her eyes, the color of onyx pebbles, so like her father's.

She gazed back at me inquiringly.

She giggled and slid off the chair. Hopping joyfully, her head bobbing from side to side, she skipped to the other end of the table to join her older sister and her friends.

"There's really no role for women in Orthodox Judaism."

I turned.

It was the women who had spoken earlier. She was a stranger, a visitor.

"It's got to change with the times or it's going to be extinguished," she said to no one in particular.

"It says in the torah," she said excitedly, "that women are lower than slaves."

The *gabbai* turned to look at her as did the Israeli artist and the estate jeweler.

"Excuse me," said the *baal torah*. "It doesn't say that at all. What you may be referring to are the morning prayers, which by the way you are misinterpreting."

"Well, I don't think so. It's medieval. It has to change or a revolution will change it! And people like me are going to lead it. We will be heard. We've *davened* at the *Kotel*. We're going to take over the *bimah*! We're not going to sit back and take it any longer! And that *mehitzah* has to go. What's with this separating men from women? It's discrimination!"

There was silence in the room.

"Oh, where is that *mamzer* Lemelman now when we need him?" sighed the *gabbai*.

THE HAT

"De Hoot" her aunt used to call it.

The Hat.

She had never understood its significance.

She, for one, hated hats. She hated the pressure on her forehead, the heat, the splattered hair, the obscuring brims. She never understood the women who wore them. Often, their hats were more attractive than their dresses. Some wore wintry close fitting cloches, reminiscent of twenties flappers, together with trellised print dresses or robes of billowing chiffon. Others chose gay oversized colored straw hats and three piece suits of unforgiving knit fabric.

She hated hats.

Once, as she left her parents' home to walk to Sabbath services, her mother complained. "She won't wear a hat!"

Her father, no fool to her mother's concerns, said, "She has so much hair, people will think it is a wig."

The hat. The hat.

It screamed "Married!"

"Off the market."

"Taken."

She told people that her head was too big. "Seven and three quarters. Most hats are seven and two quarters. I can't find one. I'd have to get one custom made."

Sometimes she said "And I have curly hair. They just don't fit."

Occasionally, she added that she had a skull deformity, a small lump, left over from a childhood concussion. "The blood ran into my sinuses. I looked like a raccoon," she added.

The truth was she hated hats.

The young girls wore their hats like badges. The older women were grateful for their hats which obscured their sagging, pale faces and errant facial hairs.

She would never wear a hat.

The unmarried women past the age of choice, sat hatless as well. They would wear hats if they could. Any hat. Stiff berets. Open crocheted caps. Flimsy snoods. Garden hats. Lace squares. Anything. Yet, as the years went by, they also wore no hats. They faded into the Sabbath scene and sat alongside the widows sometimes helping them locate the page of the service.

The hat.

The hat be damned.

She was the same person she was before she married. She was someone who loved literature, history and art, who laughed at the absurdity of life. She would wear no hat.

Then, one day, at a time of loss, she made a pledge, a promise, she would wear a hat. But she never did. And everyday brought new loss. And she was no longer married.

Was it because she had not kept her word?

She wondered.

Would the hat have protected her?

She thought of Adam and Eve hiding from the Eternal One. .

"Where are you?" he asked, though he knew full well where they were.

A line of swaying, slender sylphs stood behind her. Alongside her, her own young daughters stood tall.

But now, they were children, their beautiful faces upturned towards her, seeking, searching for answers, guidance.

"There is nothing more wonderful than to be in love," she told them.

It was her gift to them.

"How do you know?" they asked.

"You know. When you must be with this person, you must be in his presence, when your face lights up when you see him, when your body feels warm despite the cold, snow, wind."

When you no longer need a hat.

STRANGE DAYS

The man sat in the bed of a pick-up truck, facing her.

They were stopped a traffic light.

The hot late afternoon sun beat on her windshield, creating oscillating waves that distorted her vision.

Her children played in the rear seats, strapped in for safety, bickering, arguing, demanding.

The man stared right back at her.

He was very handsome. His graying hair hung loosely to his shoulders, framing his features.

He had a noble head, similar to the statute of Augustus in the Metropolitan Museum up north.

Yet, here he was in south Florida on a street named Okeechobee Boulevard, riding in the back of a pick-up truck.

With a start she realized that he resembled a late popular singer who had died at age twenty-six, He had been found dead of a heart attack in a Parisian bathtub. Or had he? Theories abounded. They said that he had tired of the music business, wanted to disappear and staged his death. His coffin had been sealed, it was reported. Only two people had actually seen the body, one his common-law wife, who allegedly died just a few years later. Had she dissembled to join him exile?

When she had been younger, his songs, lyrics had been provocative, his looks leonine. To her, all other men measured against him, failed.

Today, as she did every day, she drove to two different schools and delivered her children, worked an eight hour day, then retrieved them. This day, she had decided to go to the market. They were out of peanut butter.

Is it possible? she thought. How? What would he be doing in West Palm Beach?

If he goes through that light, I'll never see him again, she concluded.

Where could he be living? He had been born in Florida, hadn't he? She had read it in an article. He might know his way around Florida. He could hide. Why hasn't anyone else recognized him?

She remembered the youth, her youth, wearing an appliquéd tee shirt. A slash of satin fabric. Lighting Lady, she had named herself. She danced, her body flowing with the music. Understanding for the first time, the power of hypnotic attraction.

"He hit me!"

"Don't hit your sister," she mumbled.

Had he crooked his head? Had he acknowledged her? How long was this traffic light? His smile was ironic.

"It's him!" she swore to herself.

He has gone from being the idol of millions to having no car and hiding in the Everglades.

He's so beautiful, she mused.

Why is such an attractive man riding in a truck?

She hated the south. Despised the small mindedness. The drawling speech, its violent history. Yet, she had followed her husband back to his childhood home and stayed.

She had been an urban person, loving the fast moving street life of the north.

Okeechobee.

It sounded like a fungus.

She had told him that she would try it for six months.

That had been several years ago.

Everything had changed.

She was resigned.

That night, as she danced on the stage, having been pulled up from the audience, she felt her slender body on fire. The spotlights shown on her as well as the performers.

"I want a lollipop!" her son demanded.

Wordlessly, she handed him candy.

"Not that, a lollipop!"

"Me, too!" the other child said.

She handed them what they wanted.

Don't go, she pled as the light changed and slowly, then with increasing speed, the truck moved forward into the intersection.

She followed it.

He smiled, bemusedly.

"I want pisgetti for dinner!" her daughter said.

The truck roared on.

Her eyes peered at his retreating visage.

"That's spaghetti," she sighed. "Say spaghetti, sweetie."

"Pis-ghetti."

He was a cipher in the distance.

TATTELEH

His skin was wrinkled and spotted. His thinning, long hair, once brushed carefully straight back, fell forward like some 1930's schoolgirl's bob, obscuring his sunken cheeks and black-framed eyeglasses.

"I thought he was a woman," said the seated patient. At first, I thought she was odd, shuffling heavily to a table in the recreation room, fussing with her water color drawings, noisily demanding that my sons, playing cards nearby, move a chair for her. My younger son glanced warily in my direction. I jumped up to assist her.

"Thanks, honey," she said. She explained that she had phlebitis in her leg and that she needed to elevate it. She showed me her artwork, modeled after the image on a postcard. Black palm trees were silhouetted against a fiery red and orange sky but, unlike the spiky, fluid Florida palms, the fronds were thick and immobile looking.

"It's good," I said.

Across the room I watched my husband encourage his aged great-uncle to sip food supplements through a bent straw. Patiently, he patted his pajamed back. The old man leaned forward in his wheelchair and rhythmically touched the window sill.

He had been married for sixty years. They had never been apart. They had helped raise my husband. He had played with their cat. They had taken him to miniature golf and to the airport to watch the planes. They had never had children of their own and called him their "boy".

Suddenly, I wanted to speak to this woman loudly complaining of the nurses and attendants. I wanted to forget how quickly he had faded from a jovial elder exclaiming with upraised hand and smile, "I can't believe I'm eighty-eight" to a non-communicative, sunken-eyed dying man.

We had entered his room and I could see, reflected on the glass of the framed wall print, his bare legs and back, as bedridden, he lay behind a curtain.

"Stop," I instructed my sons, holding out my hands. My husband covered his great-uncle with a blanket. He lifted him into a wheelchair and placed his glasses on his face.

"I sing," she said. "Sure, on Miami Beach, just mention my name. They all know me." She had begun to sing in Yiddish, a song about waiting for seven good years of plenty. "Bring him over here," she said.

My husband wheeled him over to the woman.

"Hello, *tatteleh,*" she said, patting his hand. She sang and sang, fluidly, with a strength that belied her asthma.

He looked up, interrupting his reverie.

He smiled.

We both sang. Nursery rhymes, comic songs, plaintive songs. My sons looked up from their game.

For a moment, all was well.

Then, he was wheeled out of the room.

The next afternoon, thick, dark clouds rumbled across the sky and strong winds leveled the canopy of the palm trees.

My daughter pointed her dimpled finger at the window and shouted "Lo-ok! Lo-ok!"

He died during the night, alone, of dehydration.

THE FESTIVE MEAL

She recalled her uncle's exclamation, midpoint in the Passover seder.

The family had gathered in her parents' Brooklyn apartment. The table
was set with white linen, silverware and gold rimmed china. The cousins sat
at a rickety card table, playing with half filled paper cups and scattered
matzha shards. The youngest, a toddler, bit on the rim of her slatted playpen
and gazed at the participants from a distance.

"Now, it is time," her uncle would slowly say in his accented voice as he
read from the *Hagaddah*, "for the Festive Meal!"

She had always thought he could have done without the entire *seder*, the
building of the cities that sank in the mud, the flight from Egypt (perhaps he
would have enjoyed the "borrowing" of his Egyptian neighbors' valuables as
"payment" for centuries of slavery), even the miracles.

He had survived Dachau, Bergen Belsen and several sub-camps. His eye
warned her that if she asked, he might just tell her what he thought of the
ritual. He took nothing seriously. He had gone into the toy business,
importing hula hoops and roller skates from foreign countries. Life, to him,
it seemed, was a random turn of fate.

Each year, the children waited for his declaration, glancing impatiently in
his direction.

Decades later, in Florida, he died of a massive sepsis in his eightieth year.
She looked at his swollen body and hands and asked herself, "How will they
ever get his wedding ring off his finger?"

Her aunt realized long before any of the others, that he was gone. His
children, came and went, grieving, yet clear in their purpose, their efforts,
moving on with their lives.

She remained consumed with the past.

A word, a phrase, a name and memories flooded her vision.

"Divorce is like cancer," the woman said.

They were at a gala dinner. Across the table a short, squat woman stared at her.

"Divorce is like cancer," she repeated as if she had coined a timeless aphorism.

She knew that the comment was directed towards her.

"My mother always said" she intoned "if you need a divorce, cut it out like cancer."

Her father raced through the *Haggadah* using odd chants, unlike those of her Israeli teachers. He impatiently listened to her recite the Four Questions that she had practiced for weeks. He did not deviate from the paper book, soiled with goblet rings and chocolate fingerprints of past years. He, who had raced across the Russian steppes to escape the blitzing tanks and planes could have turned to her and said "I, too, lived under oppression. I too, fled. I was saved by miracles." But he didn't. He reserved his history to himself.

The first year after they separated, she prepared the *seder* as usual. The children sat around the gaily decorated table and they waited.

Finally she reached him.

"I got delayed," he said, drawling his words. "I met some people. Business."

They began the *seder* without him, his seat vacant.

Her mother had purchased carp at the market and placed it in the bathtub where it swam aimlessly until she was ready to club it, dress it and feed it into the steel grinder. She molded the fishmeal into oblong shapes and dropped them in boiling water. After they had bobbed and collided for a sufficient time, she would remove them, and once cooled, slide them onto a suspension of jellied sauce. She brought plate after plate of food to the table. Brimming bowls of scalding soup, flecks of parsley and swollen carrots and fat noodles floating in the yellow broth. Broiled chicken seasoned with paprika, its skin a crisp black and brown. Crumbling potatoes. Cold compote of pears, apricots, peaches and plums. Chocolates sitting in stiffly pleated paper beds. Multicolored layered cakes. As the seder went on, wine glasses were refilled. The door was opened for Elijah. A breeze seemed to enter the room lowering its temperature. She saw the sweet ruby liquid descend in the proffered cup. Had anyone else seen it? she wondered.

"School? Why are the children in school?" her mother asked. "Isn't it the summer?"

"Mom, no, it's winter. Look at the calendar. The calendar is by the fridge. Every day when you get up, look at the date. Chanukah is coming."

"*Oh, Gott vell helfen,*" she said in Yiddish. "*Dahn mazel veln zen oyfgerekhtet.*"

Your fortune will be raised up. Righted. Justified.

Was her mother's vision like that of Joseph's the Prophet's initial dream? That he would prevail over his brothers? Or did she foretell his second vision, its message of filial sovereignty foreshadowing slavery, imprisonment and exile?

"Good-bye," she said. "I don't want to make you a big bill."

"It's free."

"It is? All right. Good Shabbos."

"No, Mom, not yet. Look at the calendar."

She was drawn to the bureau. She pushed aside her daughter's sweaters and uncovered a small pine box. She lifted its lid. The hinges were askew. Two gold rings lay toppled against each other on the maroon velvet lining, their flickering reflection dissected by the blades of the rotating ceiling fan. She ran her finger along the ridged edges of the bands.

The Jamaican housekeeper fixed their meals. The door once held ajar for the visiting spirit was locked. Her uncle's skepticism, her father's solemnity, the children's fevered efforts, all memories now.

Like the incense of the Festive Meal.

THE SCHVIGA

"The first two letters are the same as in the word 'screw,'" she said, twirling her drink with a plastic swizzle stick.

"What word, Audrey?" the other woman asked.

"*Schviga.*"

"Mother-in-law?"

"Exactly."

"Some people might say that that's Kaballastic."

"You into Kaballah now, Rita, are you?"

"Oh, everyone is studying it, going to classes."

"What for?"

"They want to get touch with their inner selves."

"And that's a good thing?"

"Audrey, you've had enough?"

Audrey pushed her bangs off her forehead, then patted them back into place.

"I don't understand the connection," she said.

"What do you mean?" Rita asked.

"Between what I said and Kaballah."

"It has something to do with mysticism. It means that nothing is there by accident."

"I could have told you that."

"But you didn't. That's also mystical."

"Rita. Stay on track."

"I am. You can't follow me."

"I was talking about my mother-in-law."

"Yes?"

"My *schviga*."

"Your *schivga*?"

"You know, my mother-in-law."

 "Mathilda."

"Her."

"You said that screw.... something about screws."

"I said that the first two letters in "screw" and the first two letters in "*schivga*" are the same.

"So?"

"Don't you get it?"

 Rita smiled and shook her head.

 Do you know Mathilda?"

"Not really."

"Well, when they do open heart surgery on her, if they ever do," Audrey whispered, leaning over the table, "they are going to find a large cavity."

"Is she sick?"

"Not yet."

"She's in great shape," Rita volunteered.

"I know," Audrey said, sitting back in her chair, "not a hair out of place."

Rita smiled. "My mother-in-law invites us to dinner. She's a great cook."

"Mathilda's refrigerator is empty."

"It can't be empty."

"It's empty. I looked."

"Nothing?"

"A jar of herring. A small one. In wine sauce."

"Maybe that's how she stays so slim."

Audrey shrugged. "I guess in her day, they didn't know anything about vomiting."

Rita's eyes widened. "Do you do that?"

"And ruin these veneers? Rita, please. Waiter!" Audrey said, pointing to her drink.

"Do you think that's a good idea?"

"Do you have a better one?"

"You have to drive!"

"I'm far from drunk. That waiter is one of the best-looking things I've ever seen.   I wonder why he is a waiter."

"Probably to make money."

"How old do you think he is?"

Rita turned in her chair.

"Don't look!"

"How can I tell if I don't look?"

"I can't believe it."

Rita lowered her chin and turned. "It's hard to tell. He's running around."

"Look in the mirror!" Audrey commanded.

"My compact?"

"No! The mirrored wall!"

"Oh."

Audrey placed her finger against her cheek and stared at the ceiling. Rita glanced at her reflection. "I'd say about twenty-seven."

"How did you fix on twenty-seven?"

"I don't know. I'm kind of psychic.

"Said who?"

"No one tells you. You just know."

"Have you ever had a psychic experience?"

"Well, yes. I just had one this morning. I called my cousin and she said that she had been on a cruise and I told her that I had just been on a cruise."

"That's all?"

"No. I told her that I had seen a certain gemstone that is very popular and she told me that she had just bought a six carat ring."

"So?"

"I guessed it! It was on her mind and I guessed it."

"That makes you psychic?"

"Sure. What else is it?"

"Being psychic involves a little more. Like helping the police find a body."

"That's a criminal psychic. I just do simple things."

"Like jewelry?"

"And dishes. My cousin and I have the same stoneware. Can you believe it? We picked it out separately and I saw it in her house."

"Small world."

"I think so."

"Have you ever had a vision about violence?"

Rita stiffened. "No, why should I?"

"Ever think about a body lying undiscovered for days?"

"Not really."

"Never?"

"No. Anyway, you don't need a psychic for that. The body and the apartment would start to stink after a few days."

"Not if there's nothing in the refrigerator and no internal organs."

The women sat silently.

"You can't live without internal organs," Rita said softly.

"Precisely my point."

"What are you saying, Audrey?"

"Doesn't Kaballah say something about people living who are not living?"

"You have that confused with voodoo."

"I do not. Aren't there demons in Judaism?"

"I don't know. I'm not a rabbi."

"Well there are. And my mother-in-law is one of them."

The waiter placed a tall, frosted glass on the table.

"Thank you," Audrey said, smiling.

"She's a demon?"

"I have never seen such a cute waiter. What a body. Do you think he works out?"

"You are hoping that he works it out on you."

"Rita! Wow! I didn't think that you had it in you!"

"There are a lot of things about me that you don't know."

"What are you talking about?"

"Nothing."

"Have you ever cheated on Marvin?"

"Why would I jeopardize a good thing just for a screw?"

Audrey shrieked.

"Ssh. Keep your voice down."

"Oh, they're used to me here. A screw! I never heard you talk like that. I've known you for years and you always seemed so …"

"Ditzy?"

"Rita, I never knew…"

"Waiter," Rita said, waiving. "Check, please. We have to go."

Audrey began to gather her belongings. "I have to pick up my contacts from the optician."

"Are you sure that you're going to be all right?"

"Oh, I'm fine. Tell me more about this psychic stuff."

"What do you want to know?"

"If my mother-in-law was, say, dumped in the county dump, would they be able to find her?"

ROYAL BLUE

I had never seen the color before. Yet there it was, miles and miles of deep, roiling royal blue sea. The Gulf of Mexico. I was familiar with the gray and green Caribbean. This hue was startling in its dark density.

We were on the forward deck of a cruise ship sailing to Cancun, Mexico.

The three day trip was a sudden decision. .

The wooden planks felt soft beneath my feet.

He thrust his face over the railing, the sea winds blowing his hair upright.

I stood back.

The the silken, radiant, deep blue beckoned.

We sat at a table with newlyweds.

"We had once been like them," I thought.

But I knew that we hadn't.

There was a chasm between what we had been and what we should have been.

"I understand the pull of the sea," I thought. "Why sailors went to sea."

As the day wore on, he grew more and more agitated.

"Would you like to see the pyramids in Tulum? The temples?" I asked. "They have a tour."

He paused.

"I already made plans. I am going on different tour."

"What tour?"

"I am going to tour the town."

"But the town is always there. The pyramids are unique."

"Too late."

I recalled the time we had gone to the Bahamas. I visited the pirate jail. He disappeared.

Later, the children told me that he said that he needed something for his headache and they had waited outside the pharmacy.

I took the launch to the pier.

I walked to the waiting tour bus.

The gravel flew under my feet.

The asymmetrical pyramids looked as if they had been built by a drunken architect.

Our tour guide was a tall, reserved Mexican man who spoke with authority about the ancient Mayan civilization.

I walked to the edge of the cliff.

Behind me were the crumbling temples, before me a sheer drop, pristine white beaches and the majestic blue of the Gulf.

The sun was shining.

I raised my head and looked north.

I wondered if the native people had looked out at the sea and speculate about other peoples and other lands.

"They threw people off these cliffs," I heard the guide say, "for sacrifice."

When I returned to the ship, I found my husband in the lounge, tropical drink in hand. A tiny paper umbrella, rested on the rim. Two blonde women sat on either side of him. They held drinks as well

"Did you go?" I asked.

"Sure."

"See anything?"

"Yeah."

"I'm his wife," I said, thrusting out my hand.

 I could see raindrops begin to strike the large windows in the bar.

"Tiffany," said one woman.

"Bethel," said the other.

 No hands were offered.

"Bethel," I said, "That's a nice name. Biblical."

They remained silent.

"See you later," I said.

I passed the newlyweds as I exited. They were standing before an oil painting on an easel.

"It comes with a certificate of authenticity," said the saleswoman.

"But eight hundred dollars," the man said.

"It will increase in value."

"Honey, if you want it."

I glanced at the image.

It was a portrait of a clown. White-faced. Red nose. Wig. Satin costume. Yellow and red. Large pompons rode vertically down the chest.

"It isn't worth it," I wanted to say, but I walked on.

I took the elevator to our deck and entered our cabin

I lay on the narrow bed.

I entered the bathroom.

His electric razor lay on the shelf.

I touched it.

I looked around.

His shirt lay on the floor.

I picked it up and placed it on a hook.

I brought the shirt to my face and inhaled his scent.

"Trapped in a cabin, trapped in a cabin," I thought, "while the blue sea swirls around us."

"Where is it?" she asked.

"What?"

"Shelter Island."

"I don't know. Somewhere up in New York. On Long Island. Why?"

"I like the name."

She turned her attention to the carrot she had placed on the wooden cutting board. She repeatedly lowered a large, sharp, silver knife, comforted by the rhythmic sounds of steel against fiber.

"How many of those are you cutting?" the other woman asked.

She laughed. "I don't know. I get carried away." She looked up and stared out of the kitchen window at the wide lawn.

"We had it fixed after the last hurricane," she said.

"What?"

"The fence. I had it fixed. I'm just waiting for the next one."

"We lost three trees."

'It was awful. It undulated, like a wave. Back and forth. There was nothing I could do. The children slept through the whole thing. I was wondering if I would be like Dorothy in the Wizard of Oz."

"Are you going away at all?"

"I can't. No time. They return in a week."

"How does the little one like camp?"

"She loves it. She said that next summer she wants to go for two sessions." She scooped up the vegetables and threw them into a pot of boiling water. "Sometimes, I use leeks. It gives it a distinctive taste."

"What are you going to do with all this chicken soup?"

"What do you mean?"

"You are just making tons of it."

"Freeze it. They will eat it over the year."

"I'm sure."

"Did you want to do something today?"

"Not really. I just stopped by to give you the donor lists."

"I'll write them, thanking them. Anyone new?"

"No. Same old crowd."

"I like your haircut."

The woman touched her short, shaggy locks. "You do? Me, too. I finally had the nerve to cut it all off. Fernando talked me in to it. He said it looked Grecian."

"It does."

"So what are you up to?"

"What do you mean?"

"Dating anyone?"

The woman opened the refrigerator door and removed some parsley.

"You should put that in at the last minute. It tastes better."

"You think so?"

"Definitely."

"Coffee?"

"Thanks. I'll get it myself." She rose and removed the glass carafe.

"That one has some chocolate it."

"Even better."

"I found it at the gourmet shop at the mall." She returned the greens to the refrigerator.

"Well?"

"Well, what?"

"Are you seeing anyone?"

She laughed. "Of course not. No time."

"Time is something that you have plenty of."

"That's not true!"

"No?"

"Look, I don't want to talk about it."

"Why not? Why are you standing here chopping things and making enough soup for an army?"

"You don't know what you are talking about."

"I don't?"

"No."

"Since Mom died, I have been the only one to tell you the truth."

"Stop. Stop right now. I don't have to take your advice. I know what I am doing."

"Do you? You married a jerk and you are still mourning over him."

"I am not!"

"No?"

"It was the greatest thing that every happened to me, getting a divorce."

"So?"

"It's not that easy. Every day. People, people that knew him years ago, as a child, they say, they said, just the other day, that the youngest one looks just like him."

"And?"

"He doesn't even know it. He hasn't seen her in years."

"You feel sorry for him?"

"Yes."

"After all he did?"

"Yes. He wasn't always like that."

"You are as insane as him. Dad was right."

"You don't know what you are talking about."

"I am sick and tired of you saying that, thinking that you are the only one that knows anything."

"You have no right to comment on my life. You are not in my shoes."

"I wouldn't want to be. You do nothing to help yourself."

She turned in a fury. "I never asked you for anything. Except once. That one time in the hotel when I asked you to help me. You refused. I didn't understand it then and I don't understand it now. He was my husband, the father of my children."

"I hated him."

"But you had no right. He never did anything to you."

"I never liked him."

"That's not the issue. You turned me down. And things just got worse and worse."

"You're lucky to be rid of him."

"But he's not gone! He's alive and no one knows where he is and every time I look at his daughter, I see his face. His eyes."

"You're still in love with him!"

"No, I'm not!"

"Look, the lawyer called me. Dad's estate is ready to be distributed."

"I don't care."

"You want anything? Any dishes or anything?"

"Keep it."

"Something?

"You took care of them, you keep it."

"Fine."

"The horse. The crystal horse. They bought it when we were young, before they moved to the big house. I remember it. It rose on its rear legs. Its muscles were so well articulated. I would like that."

"I gave it away."

"What?"

"I gave it to the maid."

"Why?"

"You weren't there. I did everything."

"You should have asked me."

"If you wanted to have been involved, you should have been there. I did everything by myself."

"All the pictures?"

"In boxes."

Suddenly, the sound of sizzling steam whistled loudly.

She lowered the temperature on the range.

"It's all gone."

"What?"

"Everything. Everything we knew, had. Gone."

"Oh, you. You are so dramatic. All you ever did was live in a fantasy."

She turned and leaning against the sink, took a hard look at the other woman. She touched her sternum, gently massaging the membrane between her ribs.

"At one time, you were my idol. I looked up to you. I never wanted anything more than to be your friend."

"Look, I have to go. I have a golf date."

"Sure."

"I'll have the lawyer call you about the estate. There's cash. I'm sure you can use it."

"I'll give it to the children."

"Keep it for yourself."

"I don't want it."

"Suit yourself." She rose, picked up a large black leather bag and slung it over her shoulder. "It was on sale at Rowley's."

"Nice."

"I bought two. I gave one to my sister-in-law."

They stared at each other.

"Even she can get a date. And she's older than you."

She turned and left.

HIS DEATH

They drove up to the house.

The structure remained unchanged from the first time she had seen it as a young bride. Harsh scrub grass sprouted on the attenuated lawn. The same Chinese lion squatted beside the cinnamon colored door, its twin forever lost. The low overhanging roof dripped fat Florida raindrops on the heads of visitors.

She was dressed in black.

Tall, strangely fragile, she was consumed with grief, not for the dying man, but for herself.

She accompanied his elderly aunt. The woman had asked her to drive her to the house.

She wondered if she would see him, her husband and the father of her children.

She crossed the threshold.

The interior was dark and humid. Immediately to the left of the entrance was an étagère with figurines, mugs in the shapes of pirate heads and fading photographs. She recognized an image of her older son holding a rubber duck. He had been wailing. Then, someone handed him a toy and he smiled. Though he looked joyful, his eyes glistened with the remnants of tears. They haven't removed the pictures yet, she thought.

She walked in. Quickly, she realized that her husband was not present. She was grateful. They would stay a while and then leave.

His sister's boyfriend sat before a television set watching a prairie dog was chasing a rabbit.

In the kitchen, his father's second wife, smoked a cigarette as she leaned against the counter. Her heavily made up teenage granddaughter was speaking to her son, her husband's half-brother, a passive young man.

The aunt and uncle had been married for sixty years. She called him "Gig". He called her "Doll". In her own, non assuming manner, the way of many women who are underestimated, she understood much.

"Where is he?" his aunt asked.

In his bedroom, she was told.

"You go," she said.

She walked slowly, drawing her breath. She hated illness and death, shunned hospitals, medical equipment.

The last time she had seen him he had been sitting in the same chair that the sister's boyfriend occupied. He had been a strapping man. Six foot two. Swarthy. But he smoked. Rolling vapor would exit his car as he stepped out. He would light one cigarette with the stub of another.

She had read his medical records. Black artifacts. Tar. Emphysema. Cancer.

She wondered what it had been like for her husband to have had him as a father.

Sensuous. Lethargic. An attraction for women.

Her husband told her that he had no childhood memories save one. Early one morning when he had been about eight, fishing pole and bait bucket in hand, he started out for the oceanfront pier adjoining their family's hotel and found his father and a strange woman having breakfast in the coffee shop.

"That's her" he said years later as she flipped through family photographs. She had short hair, cut in the "avocado" style popular at the time and promontory bosoms. She wore a tight iridescent, bare shouldered dress. Her hands were placed on her hips. Her arched eyebrows seemed to go on forever. Her name was 'Peaches'. She had been a dancer in a nightclub.

She entered the room.

He lay in a hospital bed.

It was the first time she had ever seen him lying down.

"Stanley?"

His eyes remained closed.

The air conditioning compressor jostled into motion.

She realized that there was someone else in the room. A woman. A member of his wife's family.

They nodded at each other.

"Is he…?" she asked.

"We give him drugs."

She wondered if he could hear them.

The woman rose and walked out.

He resembled her husband or her husband resembled him. The great genetic amalgam. Her husband had inherited his black hair and stature and the delicate features of his sylphlike mother. He had neither of their personalities. His mother was a virago, his father wore the same bemused expression as long as he was alive. Had she really thought that? she wondered. He is yet living. With a start, she wondered if she had ever really known him or her husband.

She wanted to flee this house, her house, this town, her memories, her failed dreams, yet she was rooted in the cold, damp room, needing to understand what had happed to them.

"Stanley?"

Her eyes filled with tears.

She heard the voice of his granddaughter in the other room. She was making plans to go to the movies later that night. The sounds of the television broadcast resonated.

He had been the son of an industrialist. A tough Russian immigrant. Tall and dusky as well. None of her own children were dark, except the last.

"I'm sorry," she said.

He remained immobile.

"I'm sorry we weren't closer."

She recalled his phone call weeks earlier. It was one of the few times he had telephoned in her long marriage.

"Get as far away from him as you can," he said.

She had sat numbly on the side of her bed, the sunshine streaming though the blinds and felt her heart pound.

She stood and wept.

She said a prayer, silently at first, then aloud.

She recited an affirmation that she used to say every night before she fell asleep. That there was one God. And that people, the nation, should listen, hear. She hadn't said it in a long time.

She turned and walked out.

THE GET

She woke up that morning and something propelled her to pick it up.

A *dibbuyk*, a spirit. But wasn't a *dibbuyk*. It was something else. She had to retrieve it but she wouldn't. And then, that day or the day before, she realized or convinced herself, that it was hopeless.

She took her daughters with here because it was Sunday and she had no place to leave them or she hadn't tried to find a place.

She told them that they were going to the Metro Zoo in south Miami. They laughed with anticipation and excitement.

They watched the agitated tigers pace around an algae streaked structure and waved at the orangutans idly swinging in truck tires suspended from horizontal cables.

"You can't do it," she taunted herself.

"I have to stop and see a rabbi in Miami," she said as they exited the zoo.

They were accustomed to her visiting rabbis when they traveled.

"Do we have to wear a dress?" they asked.

"Not this time," she said.

She found the world story structure and parked. She pulled a skirt up over her shorts in the synagogue parking lot.

"Can we come in with you?" they pled as she opened the door to the building.

She didn't tell the older one why she had gone until the next year. She never told the younger one.

Afterwards, she traveled back on the interstate. Her unwieldy SUV sailed along the highway as if it were driverless.

Had this really happened?

Three strange men had watched her.

She was told to put her hands out, palms up.

The ritual was centuries old.

She stifled a cold sob.

Who were these people?

Why was she here?

Still, she went forward.

A *get*. The Hebrew word resembled the English verb to obtain, receive And yet, the Hebrew meant to break apart. To separate. Can one receive a splitting apart? She wondered.

She followed the instructions. When the rabbi wrote his Hebrew name on the document she proudly added "*HaKohain*". The *kohanim* were the priestly class. Their sons were *kohains*.

Had the rabbi said that she could never remarry him? Even if he hadn't, she had already known that Jewish law prohibits a *kohain* from marrying a divorcee. Even his former wife.

"Do you know what it is said about the word *get*?" an elderly woman in her study class had once asked her. "The letters *gimmel* and *tet* never appear together in the Torah. *Get* represents separation. It is written that the altar cries when a man divorces his first wife."

Their lives together began when he appeared in her graduate school class wearing a *magen david*, a "Shield of David" impressed on a metal ornament hung around his neck.

"You are Jewish?" she asked, finger pointing.

He had black hair. His arched eyebrows framed his large almond shaped brown eyes. She had thought he had been Greek. The town had many Greek and Italian people.

She had never thought he was Jewish.

Now, it was Jewish law that would cleave them apart forever.

"He is now a stranger to you," the rabbi had said.

"What does that mean?" she thought wildly.

In months to follow, she would repeatedly tell herself, "He is now a stranger to you."

In the past, she had rushed to forgive, comfort, reconcile. Now she found herself saying "He is a stranger to you."

The synagogue was bare. The air was moist and warm.

"I am looking for the rabbi," she said to a man mopping the floor.

"Over there" he answered in his Spanish accent.

She knocked on the door.

She heard a voice.

"Come in," it said.

A man sat at a desk, surrounded by books.

The girls peered around her body as she attempted to block their view.

"I called this morning," she said.

"Yes, come in. The witnesses are late."

"Is there somewhere my daughters can wait?" she asked.

"They can stay in the library."

The rabbi never asked the reason for their separation, if there was a chance of reconciliation, if she was certain of what she was doing.

The witnesses arrived.

The rabbi read from a preprinted form.

She recalled their *kettubah*, their marriage contract, written on parchment. Her Holocaust survivor uncle, now gone, had signed it. The framers placed it against blue velvet matting, the color of generations of skullcaps. When she sought a divorce, she hid it under their bed, afraid of its gaze.

She was told to take three steps forward.

The men rose alongside her in the narrow office.

She recalled their wedding.

They stood under an arch of cascading tangerine, lemon, ivory flowers. She circled him seven times, holding the hem of her gown.

The ceremony sped along, then the rabbi asked him if he wanted to marry her and he answered, loudly, "I do very much."

The audience laughed.

She felt unease.

Robotically, she completed the instructions for receiving a *get*.

Still, the rabbi had not asked a single question.

She longed for a paternal comment, a word of compassion.

Finally, *get* in hand, she turned to leave.

The rabbi spoke.

"So," he asked, "are you dating?"

THE POTATO EATERS

Time had stopped.

What was it about the new courthouse that so annoyed her?

She recalled the old courthouse.

A wide, shaded portico girded its façade. Fluted columns rose past the double doored entrance to a triangular pediment. Waves of ochre colored barrel tiles covered the roof.

They would enter the building daily, briefcases in hand, she in her white suit, he in his stiffly laundered shirt, blue, with buttoned down collars. He was slim and tall. His black hair glistened in the sun.

He had wooed her with stories of the sea, adversity and hurricanes.

He seemed without cares.

They would get married.

They would find jobs.

They would be happy.

She believed everything he said and followed him south.

As the months passed, she watched him become restless. He made decisions that seemed impulsive. Then, they would be together again, planning their futures, naming their imaginary children.

"Good morning," he said each day as they awoke.

"Reach for the sky," he said, raising her hands to the ceiling.

He would place her arms in a right angle, one hand grasping the anterior of the opposing elbow.

"This is how you get lifted into a boat," he said, as he pulled her to her feet.

He announced that he was leaving for lunch. She bent over her swollen abdomen to tie her shoe laces. She watched as he and another man, grinning, let the elevator door slowly close before them.

The doctor was in the corner of the room. He was washing his hands.

"What was it?" she asked

 A boy, she was told.

"He'll be so happy," she said.

And there he was, holding their son, his strong arms containing him, cradling him.

She watched the infant as he ate, gurgled and slept. She would stand at the side of his crib, waiting for him to stir so she could play with him. He rewarded her by being a responsive baby, his dark eyes, so like his father's, observing the world.

She soon realized that she could never leave them alone.

Once, as she sat at their dining room table, exhausted, she saw him stroll out of their bedroom.

"Where's the baby?" she asked, rapidly.

Thump.

Another time, she returned home and found the air heavy with sickening, sweet smoke. He lay in bed, eyes bulging. The baby sat beside him, leaning forward, his pudgy arms supporting his weight.

"How could you?"

He gazed at her menacingly, frightening her.

The child stared at them but did not cry.

She felt herself weighted down by sadness and disappointment.

How could he not see?

The old courthouse had had better light.

Tall windows, once needed to dispel the heat, brought torrents of bright sun into the rooms. The bailiff would hand the lawyers the court files as they strolled in and greet them by name, patting the men on their backs and calling the women "Ma'am".

It had been different then.

The judge sat behind a raised polymer desk.

Carpet and upholstered walls baffled the sounds.

She watched the black hands of the large, white-faced circular clock click forward.

She rose.

"We are ignoring the elephant in the room. Whether he had the capacity to hire an attorney," she said.

Silence.

"Here is a copy of the court order in which Your Honor ruled that he undergo an independent psychiatric exam."

No one stepped forward to take the paper.

"His lawyer attached stacks of medical records to my deposition reporting psychosis, aural hallucinations, etc."

Nothingness.

"He charged him forty percent of his net worth as a fee. Under the circumstances this was a violation of Rule Four, prohibiting the charging of excessive fees."

Finally the judge spoke.

"I can't help who you or your husband hire," she said. "You should know that. Anyway, his lawyer already admitted that he has a problem."

No one stirred.

"Anything else?" the judge asked.

She resembled one of the figures in a famed painting.

Silent peasants gathered around a table, partaking of their simple meal, isolated from each other and the observer. Browns and grays, the same tints as the soils that they tilled, dominated the painting. The walls seemed to touch the figures as they ate. In a world that contained sweet cream, cognac, spun sugar, butter, all sorts of fowl and viands, the family ate tubers.

Oh, the sounds and visions that must have whistled through his head, she thought.

"Will the children ever forgive me?" he had asked in a moment of calm.

She recalled the face of their son, when as a boy, he gazed at his father. He put his dimpled hand to his mouth. The summer sun shone on his damp hair as he sat alongside the camp swimming pool, waiting for his turn to participate.

And then, his father had appeared.

Through downcast eyes, she observed his fingers, grown thickened and clubbed. She recalled the strength of his hands around her neck, the hollow sound of her skull hitting the wall.

There was an anaerobic stillness in the room.

She gathered her documents.

She exited, letting the doors swing softly behind her.

    Harsh rays streamed through the exterior glass walls of the building, echoing off the speckled marble floor and metallic fixtures in the corridor.

    She raised her eyes, momentarily blinded and then instinctively, began to walk.

ENTER /CLICK

One day, she discovered internet pornography.

A New York Times article referred to a pornography web site. If The Times listed it, she reasoned, it couldn't be too bad.

The last time she had seen pornography, her college friends had pulled her into a movie theater and giggled, as she covered her eyes, occasionally peeking between her fingers.

She thought the actors unattractive and the experience embarrassing especially since a young man she was interest in was sitting right next to her.

Over the next few years, she married and had children.

Neither she nor her husband were attracted to pornography.

No such material entered their home.

Then, one day her eight year son announced that his friend had bought a Playboy magazine to school and had shown it to the other children.

"It had naked girls," he confided.

What was she to say?

His future relationships, his success as a spouse, parent and citizen hung in the balance.

"Those," she said slowly, "are poor girls."

He left, satisfied.

Then, that day, years later, she read the newspaper article about a new website.

She typed the web address and pressed the "Enter" key.

Blazing colors, luminescent images filled the screen. She scrolled down.

Hundreds of pictures of people exhibiting body parts generally only known to doctors, were freely accessed by viewers everywhere.

Some of the women were exquisite..They were so perfect that it seemed that they would be indifferent to most men.

Hirsute, well muscled men who looked as if they could lift the front end of a medium sized car were engaged in acts with other men that another generation's comedians had described in terms of pleading boyfriends and reluctant girlfriends..

Toys. Bottles. Battery operated missile-shaped objects. Cartoons.

Self-help links. Instructional sites.

After a while, the women pulling their sex organs like bat wings, their bald nether regions resembling wounds, the group sex in shabby apartments, the headlights of passing traffic visible through the narrow blinds and the forced bonhomie began to be wearying.

Pornography was racist, she decided. Photos of long haired, Caucasian girls predominated.

It was sexist. The men's faces were often obscured with hats or were out of range while the women's faces were the subject of tight focus.

She forged on.

A milky skinned woman with eggplant shaped breasts and an enthusiastic man stood upright in a woodland clearing.

Leafy green trees surrounded them.

Finally, they tired of their position. He lay her down on a bare tree stump and began to have intercourse with her.

The female's posterior pounded repeatedly against the raw wood.

Horrified, she wondered if there had been alcohol and tweezers on the film set.

She ended her on-line review.

The women truly had been impoverished, she concluded. They had lost their expectations, as had the men.

Pornography demanded hard labor by sexual workers and lonely participation by the glassy-eyed observer. Its message, direct and subliminal, was one of isolation.

With just a depression of one's index finger, one could enter the intimate world of a stranger and on and on, visiting new friends all over the world.

It was facile.

After all, hadn't she just clicked on?

DREAMS

"Dreams tell the future."

The children looked at her blankly.

"You know, Miriam and Aaron could only receive messages from God through dreams. Moshe spoke to him directly. Face to face."

She sat up straight.

"Did you know how the Delphi oracle received messages? You took Greek mythology, Jessica, you know."

"Through hallucinogens."

"Right! They inhaled vapors and went into a trance."

The younger girl stared at the window.

"I had a dream that bothered me for years."

They both turned to look at her.

"I killed my father."

Their eyes widened.

"I did. I didn't realize it at the time. Dreams represent the unconscious. You can't control them. I was angry at my father and I killed him."

"You did?"

"You know what Westerns are?"

They nodded.

"When I was growing up, Westerns were very popular on television and in the movies. They represented an American ideal of democracy. Did you know that the Western states were the first to give the women the right to vote? And they refused to endorse slavery. The eastern cities were crowded. The idea was buried deep in the American consciousness that if things just got too bad, you could pick up and move. Then one day, when the railroad was completed across the continental United States, the frontier had ended and there was a letdown in the national psyche. That's why Westerns were so popular. In books, movies and later television. They maintained that ideal of unrestricted freedom."

They remained silent.

"I loved this television program about a wagon train. Each week they showed stories of people traveling West on these things called Conestoga wagons. They were led by this figure, this actor. He was so patriarchal. He was fair. He made reasoned decisions. He was so unlike my father who was arbitrary and judgmental. I loved my father, though. He was very self-sacrificing."

The older girl watched her steadily.

"In my dream, my father was pounding a stake into the ground. I must have been seven or eight at the time. He was going to fasten the guy lines to secure the tent. We were going to spend the night in a canvas tent. And he hit it. Hard. He leaned over. And he kept on going into a large hole in the ground and I shouted 'Daddy! Daddy!' I woke up crying. I was afraid to go to sleep for years. I was afraid that I would have that dream."

She sipped her tea.

"I realized that I had killed him because I was mad at him. Because he had been unfair."

"I wish…" the first girl spoke.

"What?"

"I wish that I had had a father so that I could have given him a Father's Day gift."

The three of them sat, each consumed with her own thoughts.

“I understand,” her mother said.

“Yesterday was Father’s Day.”

“I know.”

“Why didn’t you mention it?” the younger girl asked.

“Your father was one of the handsomest men I have ever seen.”

“You’ve said that before,” the elder girl said.

 She smiled, warmed by the memory.

“That’s all I wanted to say,” her daughter commented.

“I wanted to ride a wagon west. I wanted to be a Jewish member of the wagon train. It would have been hard to keep kosher. But we would have managed. The wagon train was welcoming. They accepted everyone. “

She smiled.

“Imagine. I had a real crush on that actor.”

“What kind of crush?”

“Not that kind. Just one of admiration.”

“I would have made him a card,” the younger girl said, “if we knew where to send it.”

“He has an address.”

They stared at her.

“How do we know whether or not he’s dead?” she continued.

“He’s not dead.”

"Do you think someone would have told you?"

"I think so."

"He might as well be dead. He left me."

They sat in silence.

"I think that it's stopped raining."

She rose.

"Let's go shopping! It's senior day and I get a ten percent discount. They had better say 'No, it's impossible. You look too young.'"

"I need camp clothes."

"I want to get some new jeans."

"I wonder if I would have worn pants on the wagon train. I'd hate to have had to drag around in those long skirts. And those bonnets were hideous! Did you see that book that I have about tribes of the West? It's right next to the genealogy book. I know one thing. I would have been very self sufficient."

"Could you fish?"

"I'm sure. And that bow and arrow thing. I won ribbons in archery at summer camp."

"You did?"

"Absolutely."

"We could have made it together," the younger girl said.

"Yes. We could have."

She gave each of her daughters an embrace.

BOCA TALE

The currents in the man-made lake flew swiftly by, driven by the wind. It was the end of the year and up north, from where they had all originated, the airports were closed due to snow.

"He said that he saw them throw children on the burning wood in the trench."

The women sat on opposing leather couches as their daughters, aged seven through ten, played computer games in the other room. She realized she was unaware of what her child was doing or looking at or whether she could overhear them, but hypnotically, she continued to listen.

"I never heard that," she said turning her attention to the speaker. "I heard that he saw children die but I never heard that he saw them burned alive."

"He told me."

"He never used to talk. Once, when my older kids and I were visiting, I asked him 'Uncle Moshe, how come they never asked you to testify at the trials after the war?' He couldn't answer me. He just choked up."

"Later, he told me snippets."

"Go on," the third woman said. She was the daughter of Americans and somehow she found herself involved in their family's stories as if they had been her own. She knew the names of their aunts and uncles and their countries of birth.

"Your father was there from the beginning. He built Auschwitz."

Her daughter wandered into the room and they fell silent. Soon, she left and sat in the solarium and began to work on a jigsaw puzzle, her graceful brown legs crossed under her, her profile so resembling her father's, turned to the side.

"He said that they had marched them outside the camp and ordered them to dig a trench. They had to haul wood and throw it into the trench and then it was lit. Trucks came with children and the children were thrown alive into the pits."

"I never heard that," she repeated as if trying to distance herself from the image.

"How did he stand it?" the other woman said.

"He said that his best friend couldn't take it and threw himself into the flames. The only thing that kept him from doing the same thing was the thought that his wife and son might still be alive."

"Auschwitz was built by the inmates," she hurried to add, as if possessing historical knowledge might somehow explain the horror of the death camp. "Her father was there from the beginning. My mother said that he built Auschwitz."

"His son's name was Wolf."

"I never knew that," she said, weakly.

"Why don't you move down here?" the third woman asked.

"That would be great," she added.

"It's possible," her cousin said. "Did you see the picture of her father? It's the last picture we took before he died."

She still wore her wedding ring. A simple, gold band. Her skeletal fingers shot forth from her small hands.

"You can always call me," she offered, rubbing her foot.

She smiled.

"You know, one thing I was always jealous of!"

The two other two women paused, waiting to hear what she, who had always appeared so confident, had envied.

"You both have family or in-laws near you. I have no one down here. I was at someone's house the other night with my older daughter and the husband's parents were there, so loving and attentive. My former mother-in-law, well, I was in schul a few years ago, in the beginning, and someone asked me 'How are you?' and I blurted out 'How can I be? She's still breathing.'"

The other two women laughed.

"Your mother saved my mother's life. Without her, I wouldn't be here. "My mother had given up," she told the other woman.. "The violence. The sadism. The starvation. She was nineteen, an orphan. Her mom gave my mother her bread. She said 'Take it. I'm not hungry.' My mother said that her mother had been so hungry she could have 'eaten it with her eyes' but she knew that my mom was losing her spirit."

"How is your mom?"

"She tries to get off the phone within a few minutes. She says 'Here, speak to your father.' She doesn't want to upset me."

"Is any of the medication working?"

"She just started on a new one. My dad said that it helps with the agitation at night. Can you imagine? She knows that she has short term memory loss and she doesn't want to upset me."

The girls were seated before the computer in another room. The husband of their host had used it as an office. His books lined the walls.

Not one had entered their room, seeking food, a drink, activity. They were strangely quiet.

The dog ambled over to the television and looked up.

"He can shut off the TV. I should videotape it and send it to that TV program," she laughed, then turned to the other two women. "I don't know how people can do that to other people."

"Look at Africa."

"Look at the Middle East. There are people today who deny the Holocaust."

"My mother was forced labor. She made hand grenades. She told me the name of the camp and I thought she had gotten it wrong because I could never find it. It turned out that she was right. It was a sub camp of Gross Rosen. She was right about a lot of things."

"Does your daughter ever hear from her father?"

"At least you have good memories," she said, awkwardly, shaking her head.

"I think the three of them will be friends for a long time."

"I hope so. We have to go."

The women stood up. Their daughters surrounded them like sentries and sorting themselves out, they all made their good-byes.

"Wait, Hannah, show them your new trick."

The girl brushed her silky black hair behind her eyes, waved her spidery arms in large circles and smiling, her ivory teeth shining in her caramel colored skin, flipped backwards on a short carpet.

They clapped.

"She's going to the state championships."

"Fantastic!"

They walked out of doors.

"You know, I think I always knew, subconsciously, that I would have to raise her by myself," she said to her cousin. She stared at her daughter. "When I knew I was expecting, I called my Dad and told him 'Dad, I'm pregnant'' He said 'That's all right. Sara was ninety.'"

"Funny."

"I was immediately certain that everything would be all right."

She looked up. Soft, cushioned clouds floated overhead.

She breathed deeply. Gardenia and jasmine scents surrounded her.

She bent down and dipped her fingers in water trickling from a feebly spurting sprinkler head.

They embraced and separated.

THE WIDOWER

There he was on her monitor.

A huge, hulking man.

The photograph was underlit and of no artistic significance.

He had gray hair, closely cropped.

He wore a jacket and a tie.

She moved on.

Scrolling down, she found shots of men in black wet suits, Rubber-framed visors compressed their eyes and noses. Ribbed tubing trailed from their rigid mouthpieces.

They might as well be seals, she thought.

She passed gloomy-looking men with haggard faces, fat men with apple cheeks, bearded men, men posing in front of waterfalls, one leg up on a neighboring rock. Men standing next to horses. Men in tuxedos, the ghostly folds of their long-gone partners' gowns, still visible on the borders of the cropped images..

She moved on to another country.

Ah, Israel.

The men wore reflective sunglasses or squinted in the desert light. Some wore military uniforms.

She read their biographical entries.

Most identified themselves by numbers!

Was it Mideast security? Fear of appearing vulnerable, needy? Lonely? They were Israelis! They were supposed to be self-confident, even arrogant.

Why were they on a dating website anyway? Had they exhausted all the females in their own country?

She returned to her geographic region.

Dentists. Schoolteachers. A man at the wheel of a sailboat. He seemed to leer at the camera. A police officer. A tight red tee shirt revealed his massive biceps and forearms.

Someone sent her a message.

"I can take the kids, but I can't take the kosher," he wrote.

Furiously, she typed "You can pick up a woman in a bar and get a sexually transmitted disease but you can't take kosher?"

She hesitated, then sent her missive off into cyberspace.

She returned to the first photograph.

He was tall enough.

No spelling errors.

Well, that's it, she thought.

She turned off her computer.

She went into her bedroom and lay down on her bed.

In the dark, she stared at the ceiling.

When they had planned this room, they had decided on a southwestern motif.

The last time he had visited, he passed their bed and said "This used to be my bed".

"How did this happen to us?" she asked, numbly.

She heard the sounds of rain strike the roof. Thunder rumbled in the distance.

She spoke aloud. She found that if she said things repetitively, she could control the feeling of losing control, being drowned in memories. But sometimes, it did not work at all.

She missed the secret world that they had made for themselves. They had understood each other. Now, the few times she had seen him over the last year, his once mobile and expressive face, appeared like stone.

"I should tell you, in the interest of full disclosure, that I am not a widower."

"You're not?" she asked.

They were sitting at an outdoor café.

"No, I just put that. My wife is ill."

"Oh."

"She has less than a year to live. A neurological disease."

So did he, she wanted to tell him.

He had sunk away from them, his brilliant mind fading.

The little one resembled him.

She felt that when she held her, looked at her, her expressive brown eyes, gazing back at her, her mild olive color, a gift of his Mediterranean ancestors, she was looking at him, seven years old.

He was a nice man, the erstwhile widower.

He described his wife's decline.

He was her twin, but he didn't know it.

They both had experienced loss.

They sat across from each other, sipping iced-tea, their lunches untouched.

He never called again.

She was grateful.

THE DOCTOR VISIT

A woman driving a car passed her as she was walking across the parking lot.

She squinted at the vehicle.

She walked on. She reminded herself to order additional invitations for her daughter's upcoming party. She recalled how ethereal the girl had looked the other day as she had stepped out of the dressing room in her new dress.

Suddenly, she thought that the driver of the car had resembled her former mother-in-law.

She had not seen her in years.

She entered the facility and approached the registration desk.

Someone stepped to the right of her.

She saw gold bracelets.

She had always worn them.

Manicured fingernails.

She favored red enamel.

She continued to stare ahead at the receptionist.

"Mrs. Stein, do you have your driver's license?" she asked.

No one had called her Mrs. Stein in a long time.

She gave her the clerk the card, glancing at the photo. At the time it had been taken she was profoundly dulled with grief and fear.

It can't be her, she thought.

Then she heard her voice.

It wasn't the reedy voice that she remembered.

It was a creaking, strained voice.

She waited as the clerk busied herself with paperwork. She looked down at her open wallet. Her elder daughter's high school graduation photograph was visible. Cascading honey blonde hair trailed her shoulders. A vibrant crimson rose was pinned to her gown.

She hadn't seen or called the children since the divorce.

When her marriage was failing, she went to her and said, "Help me. Help me. The children need a father."

"No, they don't!" she had sneered.

When she had been young, she had been a fashion model. She had been slender with deep set sapphire blue eyes. Her make-up had always been perfect. Her dresses, made of expensive fabric were tailored and sharply pressed.

As the woman turned she saw that her rump, broader then she remembered was encased in shapeless pants.

They sat at opposite ends of the room.

From under lowered lids, she glanced at her.

Her face was fixed in a frozen grimace..

She looked down again.

A green suited assistant approached her.

"Your co-pay is $1,000," she said.

She heard the sound of perforated paper being ripped.

Her cell phone rang.

She took the call.

"Hello!" she said, cheerily. "Shelly Stein here. May I help you?"

She walked out of the office to answer the call.

When she returned, she was gone.

THE FLIGHT

He had the soft face of a boy raised on donuts and chocolate milk. There was sweetness about him, as if he were recalling the residue of a treat.

She looked at his feet.

He wore black velvet slippers. Embroidered multicolored garlands were visible beneath the cuffs of his trousers.

Didn't take him long, she thought, smiling.

When he had first appeared in town, unknown, his jocular, swarthy good looks waylaid fears, apprehensions.

Palm Beach was a haven for newcomers.

She had seen it before.

Some stayed, some moved on.

There were always more.

But this man, (she judged him to be in his early forties) had a quality that disarmed her.

He told stories with ease and familiarity.

He said that he was of Portuguese ancestry.

Haven't seen any Portuguese since the Red Cross Ball, she thought.

"Yes," he said. "I think we were Jews"

"Don't you know?" she countered.

"No, people forgot."

"Well, there are websites."

"There are? I'll have to look it up."

"I've heard it said in my family."

"Really?"

"I'd like it. I always felt different."

From time to time, she would hear his name, see his photographs in the society pages.

He had attended this party, that party.

Always an open-faced smile, bonhomie.

She would see him at galas.

They would embrace.

He seemed excited to see her.

She watched him move seamlessly from group to group.

He hovered around a particular womn, draped in outsized jewels and wearing a perpetually startled look, her penciled eyebrows recalling another era, another fashion,

A week or two later she read an announcement that the woman had died, aged seventy-two.

"She hasn't seen seventy on twenty-five years," her hairdresser said.

"How can someone control facts from the grave?"

"Money," he said.

"I wonder what's going to happen to her boyfriend."

"He already has someone else"

"He does?" she asked, feigning disinterest.

"A tin heiress from Peru. They are going to live here in season and travel."

"No."

"Yes. You're done!"

"How old is she?"

"Still breathing."

She rose.

"You do the greatest color. So natural."

"Less expensive than a psychoanalyst."

They walked to the reception area.

"Are you going to Animal Rescue League party with Glenn?" she asked.

"No."

"Umberto said he would meet me there. He left me an email."

"Umberto?"

"That new guy."

"Are you dating him?"

"I don't date."

"Right.. Sweetie, you don't have to marry them."

"I know."

"What is his story?"

She shrugged.

They were silent.

"Can't get my finger on him," he said.

"No, he's nice."

"You said that about your ex-husband."

They embraced and she left, smiling, looking at her reflection in the salon's mirrors.

She entered the ballroom.

She straightened her bearing.

She saw his barrel-like figure across the room.

He was talking to two women. One wore a black dress that resembled tightly woven bandages. Thick, dull, ash blonde hair framed her face. She wondered if she was wearing a wig. The other woman's backless dress revealed her skeletal ribcage.

"Look, who's here!" he said, turning to her. "You look lovely this evening."

"Thank you."

"Ladies, do you know Mariana Blank?"

"Yes, we know each other," she said.

"I imagine," he said. "You know everyone."

"Not really."

"Did you get my email?"

"Yes, thanks."

"There's a barbecue at the Rolling Hills Stables tomorrow. Benefit for Joel Hitchcock.

"How do you know everything, everyone? You've only been here a few months."

"Oh, Umberto is incredible," said the woman with the pale hair.

He smiled.

"People send me things."

A waiter strolled by with a tray of canapés.

She waived him on.

"Excuse me, ladies," Umberto said as he guided her from the group.

He sipped his drink.

"Can I get you something?" he asked.

"No, I'm all right. Still nursing this one."

"I just wanted to thank you."

"For what?"

"I heard that you told Watterbury of Prime Bank that you knew me."

"Yes, but that's about all."

"I have some funds. About two million. I would like to put it someplace safe."

"Oh, you have to be very careful," she said. "Palm Beach is full of crooks. Don't sign anything. Don't do anything without professional advice."

"I have a great team."

"You really have to stay on top of it. Examine those statements every month."

He smiled.

"You should create a trust."

"That's why I am going to meet with Atterbury."

"Watterbury."

He smiled tightly.

"Thanks."

They paused.

"Are you sure that I can't get you anything?" he asked.

"No, I'm all right."

She felt something between them. It was a maternal feeling, she concluded.

A man tapped him on his burly shoulder.

He leaned over and listened.

They walked away.

She heard the sharp ping of a metal gong announcing dinner. She looked around the room, but she had lost sight of him.

A few weeks later, she saw him in the market. He rushed in, dressed in a tuxedo, silk cravat trailing over his shoulder. He was animated, enthused.

They embraced.

"You've lost weight!" she said.

 He grinned.

"You noticed!"

"You look good."

"Thanks."

"What's new?"

"I am going to a party on the island. I came in for a bottle of champagne. What do you recommend?"

"They have a sommelier in the wine department."

"This late?" he asked, looking at his gold wristwatch.

"Probably not. Just get something expensive. How is everything?"

"Great. And you?"

"Fine."

"I've gotten involved in politics."

"I know."

"You do?"

"Yes, this is a small town. You are fundraising for the Governor."

"Right!"

"Did you ever meet with Watterbury?"

 He looked confused.

"Prime Bank?"

"Oh, no. I am taking my time. I am exploring several options. I may buy some lots for redevelopment ."

"Remember. Be careful."

"I am."

"Well , great seeing you."

"Gotta run."

He turned and walked away.

He was wearing the velvet shoes.

Do birds fly? she asked herself.

Of course, birds fly.

Not all birds fly. Penguins don't fly. He was a penguin. He was round. He wore a black suit. A white shirt. Stiff. Little ebony dots studded his chest. He didn't have orange feet. He had black shoes.

She lowered the newspaper.

She had gone out on the driveway, early, before the joggers, down, down, the long curving driveway and picked up the plastic wrapped paper, folded in thirds. She read the headlines. The carbon letters screamed "Man Kills Self in Palm Beach."

Thirty-two years old.

Profession. None. Creditors. Debt. Fraud. Conviction. Girlfriend. Murder.

Girlfriend? she thought wildly. Murder?

"He stepped off the balcony of a tenth floor oceanfront condominium," the paper reported.

He tried to fly and he couldn't fly, she thought.

Her cell phone rang. She fumbled in the pocket of her robe.

"Did you see it coming?"

"I saw nothing."

"People said that he had a temper."

"I saw nothing," she repeated.

"Are you coming in for a touch-up today?" her caller asked.

THE NIR TAMID

She stared up at the tablets.

Hebrew letters were carved into the wood.

Five commandments per tablet, separate but joined. The first set referred to the laws between man and God, the second, between man and man.

She reached the sixth line.

She quickly dropped her gaze to the heavy book resting on her lap.

Parshas Yisro. The giving of the Ten Commandments.

"Why is the parsha named after Yisro, Moshe's father-in-law, who after all was a heathen, a pagan, a Midianite prince?" the speaker asked. "Why not call it *Parshas Moshe*? After all, wasn't Moshe the greatest teacher, prophet?"

No one responded.

"It's because the chapter begins 'And Yisro heard'. What did Yisro hear?"

Someone sneezed.

"Yisro heard of all that *Hashem* had accomplished for Moshe and the Jewish people and he hurried to join them. He rushed. He brought his daughter, Moshe's wife and her two sons and joined the Jewish nation. Because Yisro accepted God so readily, because he sped to accept him, he is honored by having the chapter named after him."

She read the English translation.

"You shall not kill: you shall not commit adultery; you shall not steal; you shall not bear false witness against your fellow."

She slapped the book shut. She wondered if anyone had noticed. The old woman next to her was hard of hearing. Her Irish caregiver seemed consumed with the service.

142

Adultery, she said to herself, is right up there with murder.

She wondered if he had left a message on her internet mail.

She closed her eyes, trying to block out the memories of the previous night,

She imagined that her face was flushed.

They were all the same! Adultery, murder, theft, lying. Taking one's life, one's marital relationship, one's property, one's reputation.

She shifted in her seat.

"What are they up to?" the elderly woman asked, tapping her forearm.

"I don't know. I lost track. Somewhere around here," she said, opening the book.

"When are they going to do the prayer for the sick?" she demanded, her voice rising. Her attendant put her fingers to her lips.

"I'm not sure. Soon."

"I can't walk," she said loudly.

"Maa," her daughter said, approaching.

"Ssh."

"When is it over?"

"Same time as always."

"Remember. I have to go to Jennifer's. You promised."

"Later."

"I don't know why I have come here every week."

"Do you want to sit down?"

The girl rolled her eyes and looked over at the elder woman. She made a small circle with her forefinger adjacent to her head.

Her mother coughed, hoping that no one had seen her.

She turned and walked towards the back of the sanctuary.

The strong light streamed through the tall, Moorish looking windows.

It's as if God is in this room, she thought.

What would he say?

She must choose between her lover and God.

She found herself swinging between faith in him and faith in God.

The letters above the ark seemed burned into the wood.

She knew that the plaque over the ark had been carved over one hundred years ago and had been housed in a congregation of tailors and tradesmen in the north. When the group withered, its furniture and ornaments were reinstalled here, in their assembly.

How many eyes have gazed up at these tablets, illuminated by the *Nir Tamid,* the Eternal Flame, suspended above the cabinet containing the holy scrolls, she wondered.

During the last hurricane the lamp went out, she recalled.

Thinking of him, his broad back, deeply muscled, caused her heart to ache.

They seemed so perfect together.

She stared at the tablets.

He wanted her.

Her pleas were unanswered,

What if there isn't a God? she thought, angrily.

Silence.

"Are they up to it yet?" her seat mate shouted.

"What?"

"The prayer for the sick!"

"No, I'll tell you when."

A tall man was chosen to lift and exhibit the scrolls. Some people crooked their finger in their direction. She kept her hands at her side, occasionally wrapping them around her waist as if to steady herself.

Another man placed a velvet belt around the coiled parchments. The congregation sang as he then lowered an embroidered covering over them

A sign, she thought. I need a sign.

Seated in the sanctuary, surrounded by ritual, objects, people, she felt secure, certain about herself. Outside, in the glare of the strong sun, she lost vision.

"Did I miss it?"

"Miss what?"

"What's the matter with you? The prayer for the sick!"

"I'm sorry. I wasn't paying attention."

"What good are you!"

"Mrs. Cohen," the companion, broke in, "it's coming up. Here, mark this page" she said, handing her a prayer book.

"How did you know that?"

"Oh, I've been coming for years and with Mr. Cohen before that." She smiled.

"I love your accent. Where are you from?"

 "County Cork."

"I love Irish literature."

"Ssh!" the deaf woman said.

She glanced at her watch. Eleven. Another hour to go.

"Every day is a new day," the speaker thundered.

That's for certain, she mused.

"Dysfunctional families. Excuses. No one had a more abusive father that Abraham the Prophet. His father was an idol maker. He tried to have him killed. Brothers? Cain and Abel, Jacob and Esau. Joseph and his brothers. Yet they preserved. Reinvented themselves."

She lost track of the speech, sped along by reveries of his body and power and ardency.

Her daughter returned.

"When?"

"Soon ."

She turned, frustrated and left.

She watched her daughter's retreating back, her narrow shoulders, her slender legs tottering on her first pair of heels.

"She's going to be tall," her bench mate yelled.

"Yes."

"Like her mother. Pretty."

She wanted to gather her belongings, children and flee to him but she remained seated, as if glued to the wooden bench built for the simple worshipers of the last century and those before them.

The time ticked by and still she stayed.

THE POMEGRANATE

"Listen to this," she said, as they rolled away from each other.

She had picked up a book lying on a table near the bed.

"It's from Song of Solomon."

She read aloud.

"Come, my beloved, let us go forth into the field; let us lodge in the villages."
She paused.

"Let us get up early to the vineyards; let us see if the vine flourish, whether the tender grape appear, and the pomegranates bud forth: there will I give thee my loves. The mandrakes give a smell, and at our gates are all manner of pleasant fruits, new and old, which I have laid up for thee, O my beloved."

The afternoon sun shone thrown the translucent curtains.

"The pomegranate was a symbol of fertility. It was a common image in the Middle East," she said.

He was silent.

She lay back down on the soft pillow.

The hotel provided thick, white bedding.

The linen in her home had a southwestern design of sand-colored, repeating patterns.

She turned towards him.

His dark hair contrasted against the sheets.

"This is the moment we would smoke, if we smoked," she said.

He smiled.

"I never liked pomegranates. Too many seeds."

"It's the seeds that made it fascinating."

He looked at her.

"You know what I think it means?" she asked.

"What?"

"The poem. It means that we bring to each relationship all our histories."

"What time is it?"

"Three."

"What time do you have to go?"

"Soon."

She touched his forearm.

"I don't want to bring anything into this. Everything is new."

She looked out the window.

"We can see your office."

"Yeah. We can."

She continued to stare at him.

She looked around the room. Prints of glossy horses hung on the walls, magnificent shining animals, supported by sculpted legs. Brass lamps sat on mahogany furniture. .

His body had been dense, unlike her former husband's who had been a thin man.

"It was supposed to represent the seeds of a woman."

He crooked an eye, bemused.

"Come here," he said.

He placed her beneath him and began to run his large hands over her body.

She placed her arms above her head.

After a while, they were spent.

Suddenly, she felt anxious, as if someone were approaching, would knock on the door.

She swung her legs over the bed. Her feet touched the carpet. She rooted around for her clothes.

"My children. I told them four o'clock. I have to meet them."

He stood as well.

She shyly examined his body.

He dressed quickly.

She was filled with a desire to speak, to tell him of her shock at having been with him, the sheets against her bare skin, his hands pressing her hair away from her face as he kissed her.

But she was mute, as was he.

They entered the elevator.

She trembled as she pressed the ground floor button.

"I'm going in the wrong direction," she said.

He looked at her.

"We're going in the wrong direction. I shouldn't be leaving. You shouldn't
be leaving."

The elevator door opened

People stood aside as they exited.

They stood outside the hotel, in the sun.

He kissed her.

She worried that someone would recognize him and didn't respond.

Then she turned, and left.

THE WOMANATOR

She knew that it was wrong but she desired him anyway.

Since her divorce, the fundamental moment of her life, more important than her marriage which had taken place in a blur, a numbness of non-thinking, all hopes, dreams locked away in a cabinet labeled "Future", she had been the *major domo,* the *maitre d'hôtel,* for herself and the children, while in her unconscious heart, she sometimes felt like a child herself, wanting to hide under the blanket. Yet, the needs of her children made her rise, move through life with the shocked psyche of someone who had witnessed a massacre.

She would lie in their double bed, and run her index finger across her abdomen and think. "How big is he?" She was confident that the infant would be a boy. She knew that in order for her husband to be involved in the child's life it would have to be a boy.

One day, she felt a fluttering in her lower body.

Having no one to ask, no elder woman, refusing to share her thoughts with anyone, including her doctor, she felt as if she were the only person in the world to have experienced the sensation.

He placed his ear on her abdomen.

She touched his black hair.

If she had just been able to keep him there, she later thought, close to her, listening for the heartbeat of his son, she could have protected them both.

The pregnancy was long. She passed her first due date, then her second. The summer days were hot. She refused to answer the telephone. She had no more excuses for curious callers.

Finally, he convinced her to go to another doctor. She wore her best dress, the striped one. It billowed like a tent.

She watched as he and the doctor conversed.

It was as if they were planning a fishing trip.

The next day he brought her to the hospital.

They placed her on a bed.

She stared at the pale green ceiling. She had never seen a live birth or been with an infant since she had babysat at age thirteen. Afraid to touch the child, she had stared at her through the slats of her crib as she cried. She talked to her, trying to soothe her. Finally, she fell asleep or the parents returned and she fled.

They slid a needle in her vein. A clear fluid began to drip, drip through the blue tubing, into her arm.

Within an hour, a relentless, mechanical force began in her uterus.

No one spoke to her.

The pain rose and fell in ninety second intervals.

She watched the big, round clock on the wall.

"Can we give you anything?" they finally asked.

She shook her head.

She would not harm her son.

She tried to become unconscious between the contractions. She found that if she didn't anticipate the pain, it was more manageable.

After several hours, the doctor examined her.

"You're going backwards."

"What?" she asked.

"Your cervix is swollen and is getting smaller."

She said nothing.

He approached with a long instrument that resembled a knitting needle.

"I'm going to break your water," he said and before she could respond he inserted the device in her body. Nurses held her knees.

"You're so close to the baby!" she wanted to scream but within seconds, torrents of warm fluid rushed out of her body.

For the first time, she sobbed. Her tears seemed to flow rhythmically paralleling each contractive push of her abdomen.

She said little after that.

She was silent when the doctor returned the next day, after another sixteen hours of labor and said something about "the better part of valor." She lay passively as the anesthesiologist placed a black mask on her face and asked her to count backwards from one hundred.

The doctor was washing his hands at the end of the operating room.

"What was it?" she asked.

"A boy."

She smiled, justified.

She saw her husband hold the baby, cradling his perfectly round head.

"I have given him the greatest gift," she thought.

For the moment, they were parents, creators, artists.

"I told you so," the gardener said when she called.

A tree had fallen during the night, a huge palm, weighing tons. If it had fallen backwards instead of forwards, it would have crushed her and her daughter, lying in her bed. If it had crashed to the right, it would have damaged her neighbor, a widow's house. To the left, it would have crushed her car.

"I told you them roots were rotten," he said.

"I know. I just had so much on my plate," she said.

"Well."

"I saw the green fronds and I thought it was alive."

"That don't mean nothing. It was rotten. I showed you."

"I pushed it out of my mind."

"I'll be there later this morning."

"Thanks. I appreciate it."

After they met and after months of communications, daily, multiple messages, filled with poetry, philosophy, news, expressions of passion, she told him, through tears, that she had never been married, that she loved him, was shocked that she had fallen in love with him. "Ditto," he said or something of the like. One day, he wrote "I want to make you mine forever."

Occasionally, she would see a display of his temper. Still she kept on, he kept on.

"I sailed passed every stop sign," she said as they walked in the sun, on one of his visits.

He said little but when he kissed her, the ferocity of his kisses said much.

As they embraced, that last day, on the lakeside path, she found herself looking over his shoulder down the tree shaded walkway. With a start, she realized that in the past, nothing would have come between them, that she would have barely been aware of anyone or anything else when they were together.

He resembled her husband.

She had never told him.

"How tall was he?" he once asked.

"Six, three."

She wanted to say that he had been so handsome that men and women used to turn around to look at him. Sometimes, she told the children. She wanted them to be proud of him, something to sustain them, in his silence, his absence.

She looked at him.

She had felt differently earlier in their relationship.

"I belong to you," she had said.

Then, later, after she had sent him missive after missive, describing how she felt as she had driven him to the airport and then the next day, when she thought of him and having been with him, she felt him withdraw. Her expressions of love, affection were not enough. "Don't test me!" he wrote.

She sat in her darkened kitchen.

Silence overwhelmed her.

She wondered what her son was doing.

He had been wounded by the divorce.

"You can always get another husband. I can't get another father," he said.

She recalled the day she had sat on the running board of his car, hoping to reach him, talk to him, convince him, with her saddened eyes and burdened heart. He refused to look up. Finally, he mumbled "You will always be my wife whether we are married or not."

Somehow, in her mind her husband and her lover were becoming the same person.

She found herself comparing them, trapped in a spider web of memory.

"It was them roots!" the gardener said.

He made me breathless, she thought.

"Say his name," she whispered, "that was all that I could say. Just his name, over and over again."

RAIZA

"Hello? Come see me. I am dying."

I looked at the digital number displayed on my cell phone.

"Who is this?"

"Raiza. Come. I have cancer. The doctor says I will be dead in four or five days."

Her name instantly transported me to the Holocaust world of my parents, a world that I simultaneously resisted and to which I was drawn. I would read voraciously, engage with the dwindling number of survivors and their children but I drew a line. I would never ask about what they had seen or heard or thought. I decided that I would never visit Auschwitz. I knew that sight of its narrow, rust colored bricks and the electrified fence, its concrete posts curved inward like bent fingers, so feared by my mother, would have stilled me.

"Come."

I deflected, unable to believe that someone could pick up the phone and say "I am dying."

"I want you to come to my funeral."

She went on to talk about her Italian furniture, said that it had given her cancer.

I tried to follow her, assess what she was saying.

Was it the result of drugs, mental decline?

But I knew Raiza to be highly intelligent, forceful, honest.

I had met her six months earlier when I had visited her Boca Raton condominium to interview her about an article I was considering writing on the visit of the Grand Mufti of Jerusalem to Auschwitz.

Someone referred her to me, said that she had witnessed the event.

I downloaded photos of the Grand Mufti, printed them and went to see her.

I found a small, elegantly dressed woman.

Her apartment had tile floors and plastic covered furniture.

An aide bustled in the kitchen.

We talked for two hours.

She had had many health problems but seemed to have overcome them all.

She had one son.

A doctor.

He lived in Connecticut.

She had been married twice.

She had met her first husband right after she was liberated from Bergen Belsen and had married him the same day.

"The same day?" I asked, wide-eyed.

"We were alone. We had nobody."

He had died in a car accident in Belgium where they were living at the time.

She had re-married in America.

But our first visit was not about her biography or my biography.

It was about our families.

To my astonishment and perhaps hers, she was from the same town as my maternal grandmother.

Moisei, Romania.

Her father was from my mother's town, Ruscova, Romania.

She had been deported to Auschwitz at the same time as my mother.

She had been a slave laborer as had been my mother.

I mentioned several names.

Mallek. Pollak. Genuth.

She recognized every name. She pronounced Genuth, Ghneth.

I was incredulous that I should have been directed to her at a time when my own mother could no longer talk and I continued to mourn the recent death of my father.

Her Romanian Yiddish accent was comforting, familiar.

I thought of my mother's sisters, Frida, Charna and Dvora. All gone.

How wonderful they had been to me, shielding me from what they had witnessed, loving me, delighting in me, encouraging me, offering me whatever they had, food, praise, presents.

Keep speaking, Raiza, I thought.

I showed her the photos of the Mufti.

She said that the man she saw had had a beautiful uniform.

I was confused.

Who was she talking about?

The Mufti was always depicted as wearing a tall, white turban and sweeping caftan.

She could easily have said that the man in the photograph was the Mufti and I could have gone on to write the article, but she didn't.

She was a fierce guardian of her memories, even if they didn't fit the narrative.

I didn't write the article.

She would call me from time to time.

She would wish me a Happy New Year, a Happy Chanukah, though I privately believed that she no longer a practicing Jew. She had seen too much.

Then, I received the call.

Before I hung up, I promised to come see her.

She mumbled the name of the nursing facility.

I wrote it down.

A day or so later, I looked it up. One entry resembled the name she had given me. The telephone number she had used and the listed number were the same.

Another day went by.

Sunday.

The weather was exceptionally beautiful.

"I am going to Boca Raton," I told my teenage daughter.

"Why?"

"I am going to visit a friend."

So I drove south.

I had forgotten the directions, but somehow, I found my way.

I pulled into the parking lot of a single story facility. It was surrounded by trees which had dropped their brown leaves on the lawns and walkways, where they remained, uncollected.

I hated it.

I hated all nursing homes.

My father hated the nursing home into which he had moved.

He died seven weeks later.

But I knew I had to compose myself.

I parked at the rear of the main building.

Uniformed workers sat outside, smoking.

Their rapid, loud speech echoed as they spoke on cell phones and to each other.

"Excuse me," I asked, "where is the entrance?"

One woman pointed to the back door, head bowed.

"Thank you," I said.

I walked past wheeled racks of food trays.

The sliding glass door opened.

So much for security, I thought.

I wondered why I had come.

I knew that Raiza was an insightful, exceptional woman.

When I had earlier visited her in her apartment, I unexpectedly found myself speaking of my own heartache, of the divisions in my family.

"Ssh," she said when I finished, putting her narrow finger to her lips. "There is nothing you can do about it."

We sat at her dining room table, moving from English to Yiddish and back again.

"Accept it."

I felt that the act of telling her things I had told no one, could no longer tell my father or my mother, had been a resolution.

"Okay," I said. "I will."

I went to the reception desk and asked for Raiza's room number.

The attendant pointed to her right and returned to her computer screen.

I continued on.

And there she was, sitting in a hospital bed, thin but well groomed, eating lunch.

"Here I am," I said.

She acted as if she knew that I would come.

I sat on her bed, facing the window.

"I'm dying," she said.

"No," I insisted. "It's not for you to say."

"The doctor told me."

"What kind of doctor would say such a thing?"

"Four or five days."

"Don't say that," I said. "You will invite the *Malech AmAhvis*."

So, we started to talk.

She said that she had witnessed 530 English soldiers gassed in Auschwitz. She said that hundreds of girls had been forced to march in the snow and that only 20 something had survived. Only she didn't say 20 something. She said the exact number. She spoke so much that my mind could not absorb what she said. She said that she had been the victim of medical experiments, that all her blood had been drained.

"How could you live if all your blood was drained?"

She didn't answer.

I showed her a cell phone photo of my maternal grandmother and my great-grandmother, taken in Ruscova in 1943, at a time when my mother said they were "already *auf tsouris*".

"That is exactly how my mother looked, she said, "with the *tichel*".

She spoke about her first husband, a Polish Jew. She said he looked like the American actor, "Robert Taylor", how they had waited five years until they could immigrate; how they had moved to Belgium, how she had discovered that he was having affairs with other women and how she had left him, taking their 13 year old son.

"He never wanted to divorce me," she said somewhat proudly. "I divorced him."

Her words reminded me of my now distant memories of my own marriage.

She had forgiven him, it seemed, recalled his memory fondly.

"He died in a car accident."

"They didn't have seat belts in those days," I added incongruously.

"I came here with my son. He never caused me any problems. He got scholarships."

"Eat," I said. "It is getting cold."

An aide entered the room.

Raiza spoke to her in French.

"I don't speak French," she said.

"Creole?" I asked.

"No. I am from the Bahamas. My parents are Haitian but I was born in the Bahamas."

"I speak French, Flemish, Spanish, Yiddish, Hungarian, Romanian and Polish," Raiza said, as the woman left.

What happens to all this when she is gone? I thought.

"You are a strong woman."

"I'm dying."

"You'll show them."

"I want to live," she said.

We sat silently.

"Are you in pain?"

She shook her head.

"They give me drugs."

I stood and pulled down her soft sky colored tee shirt that had risen, exposing her ribs.

I pointed to the flat screen hanging on the wall.

"Do you watch?" I asked.

"Never."

Her gray hair was beautiful.

Straight. Well cut.

She resembled Greta Garbo.

"I was 18 when we were taken away."

"My mother was 19," I said.

I couldn't imagine how she had survived.

She had seen everything, lived among the dying. What had sustained her?

"I was more dead than alive when we were liberated. On April 15."

"My mother said that her gums had covered her teeth."

"I couldn't talk."

The words tumbled out of both of us, driven by a desire to share her experiences, my recollection of my mother's history. I talked and talked. I became my mother as I sat on Raiza's bed facing the dark trees and the sunlight and the running stream outside her window.

Her phone rang.

"*Mon avocat*," I heard her say

She handed me the phone.

"My son. You speak to him."

I took the phone.

An accented voice said "Hello?"

I spoke rapidly.

"I am not here as a lawyer," I said, "we are friends". I gave him my name and phone number.

I heard his sad voice, felt his fear and love for his mother, their unique bond.

She had told me that he had been in Boca Raton with his wife and children for four days and just gone back to Connecticut.

He wasn't a sixty-something medical doctor. He was a single child of a single mother, a Holocaust survivor, an extraordinary woman.

"We're probably related," I said.

He laughed.

Children of survivors delight at that expression.

I told him to call me if he needed anything.

I handed the phone back to Raiza.

She joyfully spoke with her son.

I stood up, whispering, 'I have to go."

"I love you," she said.

SOJOURN

I left my home in West Palm Beach, FL that July day at 4:30 a.m., to catch a 6:00 a.m. plane to New York City.

I waited on line at the airport, clutching my driver's license and boarding pass in hand. Since the attack and destruction of the Twin Towers in New York, eleven years earlier, travel had inalterably changed. Shoelessness and x-ray examination were now a part of life.

I was flying north to join my youngest daughter arriving from Israel.

I expected a confused, exhausted teenager to be waiting for me at the International terminal.

Instead I found a tall, smartly dressed young woman standing there as I deplaned a domestic flight who announced that she wanted to return to Israel and join the Israeli Defense Force.

"We'll talk about it," I said.

Secretly, I was pleased.

The past year had been an increasing struggle of missed curfews, ever expanding social life, driving, and independence.

Our family had been fractured a decade earlier when her father and I divorced.

A few years earlier, I had found myself pregnant, facing the needs of a rambunctious three year old and two teenagers.

But I always knew that I would have the child and that I would raise it, alone if necessary.

She was a beautiful baby, even as a newborn.

Product of a caesarean delivery, she arrived silently and drowsily, as if she had been reluctantly awakened.

No squished ears or swollen face.

She had feathery black hair and rosebud lips.

Now, she wanted to crawl on her belly in the desert in green fatigues and carry a rifle.

"I think it's a good idea," I said.

We began our adventure.

We found the Long Island Railroad station terminal and bought tickets for Bridgehampton and waited.

We chatted. She told me of her travels in Israel, the friends that she had made.

The modified version.

Soon, we boarded the train.

In all the years I lived in the New York region, first in Brooklyn, NY, then Bergen County, NJ, I had never taken the LIRR.

I wondered at my own adolescent passivity.

My children traveled a fatherless world.

And I had been surrounded and even overprotected by my immediate and extended family.

The weather was perfect.

Sunny. Low humidity.

People entered the car.

Asian teenagers talked to each other in low voices. A long haired blonde girl in a short, tight, red dress, repetively flipped her hair.. An academic-looking couple, wearing wrinkled shorts and faded sneakers stood awkwardly as the car swayed even though there were available seats.

There were several people with dogs.

"She needs a husband," I whispered to my daughter after an hour of watching a woman, probably in her early thirties, maul and kiss her puppy,

Finally, we arrived at Bridgehampton.

My friend was waiting in her vehicle. We filled her trunk with our luggage.

The house she had rented was nearly two hundred years old.

It had narrow doorways (were people smaller then?) and creaking floorboards. The home had endured multiple additions over the years and ceiling heights varied throughout. The kitchen seemed small and inefficient. I thought of the oversized marble and granite kitchens common in Palm Beach. Gradually, the beauty of the house was revealed. It was filled with treasures. I wandered among a first edition of THE LIFE OF GEORGE WASHINGTON by Washington Irving, pewter candlesticks, antique dark wood furniture, noble staircase.

We placed our luggage in our room.

I realized that my daughter and I were to share a bed.

It would be the first time we had slept together since she was seven or eight years old.

Something had kept her in my bed, in her father's space, even though she had a room of her own.

She wouldn't go to her bed. She seemed to be afraid.

One day, she left one day and never returned.

Since she had become a teenager, she refused to let me even peck her cheek. Hugs were out of the question.

"I don't like to be touched!" she declared.

But I knew it wasn't true.

I had seen her embrace her friends countless times.

It was another loss I felt acutely.

So, I waited, until the adolescent storm would pass and she would be a loving, responsive daughter once more.

When we retired that night, she said "Put a pillow between us!"

I rooted around on the floor for a rectangular cushion and placed it lengthwise.

She didn't request it the next night or the night after and I wondered if we had crossed a threshold.

The grounds contained magnificent trees, flowers, a pool and a tennis court.

It had once been a working farm.

We decided to go to town.

I looked at my daughter's serene face as we drove and marveled at her warm skin and black eyebrows.

She had grown into a beautiful woman.

Her dark hair had been lightened by the son, their curls and tendrils sported shades of red, even honey blond.

She had a startling profile, observant brown eyes.

She was clever and self-possessed.

I sighed with gratitude.

We had come a long way.

My friend and my daughter decided to continue on to the beach.

"I'll pass!" I said.

I disliked the beach and avoided the sand, greasy lotions, heat whenever possible.

I stepped out of the car.

They went on.

I passed a church and stopped.

Its steeple rose high against the blue sky.

I had forgotten about the clarity of the northern sun.

In Florida, we never ventured outside without sunglasses.

As a result, the light always seemed filtered.

In the north, it seemed more defined.

I pushed the graveyard gate open and entered.

When I had been a child, I had been terrified of cemeteries.

My father had died in May and unwillingly, unexpectedly, I found myself standing at his gravesite. We stood, his family and friends, each in their own way impacted by the formidable man he had been, each lost in their own thoughts. We stood in a park-like setting as a balmy breeze, cooled by an early morning rain, blew around us.

Dry-eyed, numb, I followed the service. The rabbi spoke. His grandchildren spoke. I spoke.

He was buried, according to tradition, in an unpainted, pine box. His Hebrew name was handwritten beneath the word "*Rosh*" or head. Cartons of worn prayer books no longer fit for use were placed on the lowered coffin and soon, both were covered by reddish earth.

My trip north was my first venture outside West Palm Beach since his death.

I studied the weathered Bridgehampton tombstones.

Nearly all the interred had biblical names.

I recognized obscure angels.

Couples were buried side by side. Often, the stones read "Wife of…" The woman was given equal honor but her status as "Wife of" was central to her identity. The names of their children who had died in Infancy or at a young age were etched on the stones as well. Together in death. Searching the nearby plots, I learned that some of their children had survived and had lived to have children of their own.

Suddenly, I stopped..

One tall, obelisk stood out.

I read the name of the owner of the house in which we were staying.

The year of his death was 1840.

He had been a Captain.

I had visions of rum and molasses, piracy, blue and white export China.

All had transpired here in Bridgehampton.

Despite their worldly success, these people valued this small town as a new Zion and remained, in life and in death.

I felt comforted by these people's endurance, their hope for the future, their faith, their acts in respecting the dead and the living who remember them.

I felt a kinship with them, from their Old Testament names to their love of family.

I exited the graveyard and continued my tour, anxious to tell my daughter of having discovered something, smiling as I visualized telling her the story with its implication that I had been guided to the Captain's resting place by an unseen hand.

Children, I knew, even almost grown children, need a purpose, a vision and a dream.

The next morning, I woke with a start.

At home, I awakened at the same time each day.

Six-fifteen a.m.

I wondered how my body knew.

It seemed that everything in a woman's life, her fertility, childbearing was governed by time.

My daughter slept soundly, her blanket completely covering her head.

I made my way to the bathroom and showered and dressed.

My friend and I were going to religious services in a nearby town.

The sanctuary resembled a large wooden tent. Oversized fasteners and bolts connected the pitched ceiling planks. Light streamed in through sliding glass doors on either side of the room. Men and women were separated by a low, wrought iron barrier. We sat in the upholstered pews and withdrew our prayers books. The congregants sang in unison. The melodies were the same as those in our synagogue at home. A woman waved at me.

"Who is that?" I whispered..

I returned her wave.

"She was in Palm Beach," my friend said.

The rabbi sat in a slatted armchair on the podium.

The cantor stood at a raised platform in the center of the chamber and led a choir of men.

A sense of foreboding filled my thoughts.

I thought of all I had left behind,

Unfinished matters, unanswered questions.

And yet, I felt comforted by the rhythmic ritual.

I smiled, thinking that the original settlers of this town probably knew the Bible as well as anyone in the room.

People continued to arrive. Soon the doors leading to the terraces were opened and the temperature began to rise.

People fanned themselves with their programs.

At the conclusion of the service, a speaker walked up to the lectern.

He was the mayor of a large city in Israel.

He spoke articulately, using American idioms.

This is the future of Israel, I thought.

He talked of tourism, infrastructure, social networking.

The open prayer book rested on my lap.

I had barely glanced at it.

I returned it to the shelf affixed to the back of the pew in front of me.

We rose and walked outside to the veranda.

Food abounded on the tables.

Trays of rolled sushi and bowls of floating herring.

A slow-cooked stew of beans, potatoes and beef.

And on and on.

Despite, the bonhomie, I felt a malaise among the people.

The economy? Terrorism?

The service had not managed to lift their spirits.

No visions of Paradise, here or elsewhere.

I wondered what the Captain and his wife would have said.

We returned to our former farmhouse.

I strolled the grounds. I saw climbing ferns, tangerine colored flowers and mosses growing at the bases of, gnarled trees. Sunlight streamed through the overhanging canopy. The path was composed of slate panels, laid in a meandering fashion. Wooden posts connected by rows of wire encircled the property. At home, I mused, we had vinyl picket fences.

We made plans for evening.

My daughter would go out with our host's children.

My host would attend a family party.

I would remain behind.

Soon, the house was quiet.

I walked outside and found myself on the main thoroughfare. I strolled the streets as twilight descended.

I marveled at the difference between Florida sunsets and northern sunsets.

In Florida, the sun seemed to set within minutes.

If one looked away from the brilliant, fiery red and orange sky, streaked with turquoise and plum bands, it might rapidly darken in the interval, as if someone had waved a wand.

Here, in the north, the night took longer to fall.

I looked in the window of a celebrated tavern.

Patrons were lined up against the bar, drinking, chatting.

Many seemed distressed, prematurely aged.

I sat on a bench and watched diners.

Couples barely talked to each other.

They ordered and received their foods, never acknowledging each other's presence.

Yet, I spied wedding rings, engagement rings.

I thought of my former husband, how we reveled in each other's conversation and company. We were together all day, every day. I used to say "They are going to have to bury us on top of one another!"

I knew that if we had been sitting in Bridgehampton, on Main Street, as darkness approached, we would have so engaged with each other that we would not noticed and would have lit the candle in the webbed red glass jar and continued to laugh.

A bus's roar sounded behind me,

I rose and continued to walk.

Soon, I came upon an art gallery, lit from within, people milling, drinks in hand and I entered.

I stood in front of a large painting and studied it.

A short, elderly man came up beside me.

"I wonder what else he did?" he asked, in a vaguely familiar accent.

Was it Polish?

We continued to talk.

Out of the corner of my eye, I spied the tell-tale green-blue ink on his forearm.

I waited, politely.

Finally, I asked "Where were you from?"

"Austria."

And we were off.

He was vigorous, funny, clever.

He was visiting his daughter.

Soon, she came over and addressed him as "Daddy".

She was sixty, if not older and he must have been close to ninety, yet she called him "Daddy".

In later years, I never called my father "Daddy."

So much had happened, to us, between us, it just didn't seem sufficiently dignified.

The day he died, I held his bruised and torn hand, once so powerful, a hammer, in my hand, or, his nearly comatose hand held mine, for hours.

His eyes were closed.

I spoke of how proud I was to be his daughter, how much I admired him, loved him.

I felt his sprit in the room, hovering above his battered and wounded body.

I thought of the phrase in Deuteronomy describing how the Prophet Moshe's soul left his body. The sages said it was as easy as a pulling a hair from milk.

I prayed that my father didn't know what was happening.

I prayed that he was unconscious.

The nurse entered the room and gave him an injection.

Morphine?

I never knew.

She felt the pulses in his ankles and followed me out into the hall.

"He's dying," she said, not unkindly.

I thought "If I stay in the corridor, he will not die."

But he did die.

I walked back into the room and he did not look dead.

I touched his skin.

It was not cold.

So I sat, alongside his clean linen sheet and stared and stared, at the face that I had seen nearly every day of my life until I left for college, age seventeen, and on every vacation and each summer until I married and moved to Florida and on every visit thereafter, as I brought my children for his approval.

His authoritative presence filled our home.

I sat alongside his bed and spoke, calmly, as if we were sitting around the dinner table and talking about our day.

I knew that he had wanted to live, whatever his condition.

His will was that strong.

But his body was no longer able to contain his soul.

Soon, our rabbi came.

The first thing he did was cover my father's handsome face with the sheet.

And I never saw his strong profile, his intelligent brow, again.

"I was on *Sixty Minutes*," my companion said.

I didn't understand what he had said.

"Scott Pelley interviewed me."

"Who is Scott Pelley?" I asked.

"He is on *Sixty Minutes*. The story about the records."

"The records?"

"Yes, On *Sixty Minutes*."

"Oh, I saw that. Bad Arolsen. The Nazis kept records."

"Yes, that's me. I just spoke to Scott Pelley last week."

"I remember the program but I don't remember you."

"I'm in it."

His daughter walked over.

"Daddy, are you hungry? Eat this."

She handed him a mushroom in a napkin.

He ate it, smiling at me.

We walked over to another painting.

"I don't get it," I said.

"They get money for this."

"My daughter goes to an art school and they make better things than this."

"How long are you here?"

"Just a few days.

He turned to look at me.

"Are you married?"

"*Geget*," responded using the Yiddish word for divorced.

"How long?"

"Nine years."

"And you never remarried?"

"I had young children. They came first."

He was silent.

"But now, they are grown up."

I sat on a nearby desk.

"Shrimp?" a waitress asked.

"No, thanks," I said.

He took a shrimp.

"I have to go," I said, standing.

I looked around for his daughter. She was engrossed in talking to a man.

"Please say good-bye to your daughter for me," I said. Hands in the pockets of my slacks, I walked out.

"How was it?" I asked my daughter the next morning.

"Okay."

"Where did you go?"

"Sag Harbor."

"Where?"

"A club."

"They let you in?"

"Sure, why not?"

"You are sixteen."

"I told them I was in college."

"You lied?"

"Sure."

"You shouldn't lie. Didn't they ask you for ID?

She looked at me incredulously

"No."

"I knew we shouldn't have taken off your braces."

"What?"

"How did you get into a club?"

"I sat at the table."

I took a deep breath.

"And?"

"And what?"

"Did you drink?"

"Duh!"

I couldn't bring myself to ask what she had drunk. I secretly prayed that she had ordered a soda.

"Who paid?" I asked, weakly.

"I have money," she said in a huff, exiting the room.

I had lost.

We both knew it.

Later in the day, we began to pack. Our clothes were strewn across three suitcases. Somehow, we managed to close our luggage and bring the pieces downstairs. My cousin and her daughter were scheduled to pick us up at

5:00 p.m. on their way back from East Hampton and take us to their home in Bayside, New York.

We had several days of college visits planned.

We hugged our host and thanked her for her generosity and drove away.

My cousin and I had strong ties. Our mothers were sisters and survived the Holocaust together. Her mother had saved my mother's life. My mother had been unable to go on, defeated and her mother kept her afloat.

We talked and talked. We talked about our other cousins, her sibling and my own.

We told and retold stories.

We talked about our mother's oldest sister.

She had been a formidable character, with a sharp, incisive sense of humor.

"Once," I related to my cousin, "I told her that her that she was spelling her name wrong, that it was spelled "Frieda" not "Frida.

"Don't you think I know how to spell my own name?' she asked."

My cousin laughed.

"I had too much education and not enough common sense," I said.

The next day my daughter and I took the subway to Columbia University in to take a college tour. We would spend the night with my son who lived in lower Manhattan.

I had not been in Morningside Heights since I had been nineteen and had had a summer job at Columbia.

And here I was again.

I remembered the libraries.

They had been my favorite spots.

I wondered what it was within me at that time that sought out books instead of people.

My own daughter celebrated her youth, her drive, her *joie de vivre.*

The next day we visited New York University and two other colleges.

"Where do you want to go for your birthday?" my son asked.

"Some place with music."

We went to the Soho neighborhood, not far from where he resided.

A three piece band played popular classics.

My son and daughter presented me with a lithograph of Central Park and sang "Happy Birthday!"

When we left, I looked up at the surrounding buildings and breathed deeply.

The area had been the home of hundreds of thousands of immigrants.

I felt their presence.

The next day, I decided to go to synagogue near my son's East Village apartment. As everyone slept, I shut the front door softly behind me and left.

I walked through narrow streets, bustling, even at 9 a.m. on a Saturday.

The first thing that struck me upon entering the sanctuary was the odor of mildew.

I heard the sound of groaning and wheezing air conditioning compressors and felt cold air, on my neck.

I looked up.

A huge organ dominated the rear balcony, its tubular pipes rising grandly to the ceiling. Two galvanized rectangular vents stood upright on either side of it, pulsating refrigerated gusts into the room.

I was confused.

Orthodox synagogues prohibited the playing of musical instruments on the Sabbath. Why was there an organ?

"This is going to be a long day," I whispered to myself.

Bronze colored plaques lined the walls.

For a moment, I thought that I rather have read the plaques than follow the service. My former husband's ancestors had lived three or four blocks from the synagogue at the turn of the prior century and I wondered if I would find their names.

A young cantor led the service.

His blue jeans were visible beneath his prayer shawl.

The men read from the scrolled torah.

Suddenly, I recognized the slim figure of a woman, a famous actress, whom I had met in synagogue the year before. I had been standing as the ark doors opened and the torahs withdrawn and I turned. She stood right behind me, almost as tall as I, utterly recognizable. We began to talk. She also had a young teenager daughter and was a single working mother. In fact, she told me, she had a performance that night in West Palm Beach.

"Hello!" I mouthed, waving.

She narrowed her eyes, trying to remember.

"Palm Beach!" I said.

"Oh, hi!" she whispered and waved back.

As the service went on, I watched her from time to time.

She knew the prayers by heart and often swayed with fervor

As soon as the final melody was chanted, she exited her row and left.

"She probably has to return to her daughter," I thought.

"This *schul* used to be a church," an elderly man told me at the kiddish following the service. "It was a Lutheran church and then there was a boating accident and over twelve hundred people drowned in the East River. We bought it in 1940."

"There were no members before 1940?" I asked.

"No."

"Here is a history of the church," he said, handing me several sheets of paper.

"Are you married?" a man asked me.

"No," I said.

"Divorced?"

"Yes."

"Who filed?"

I grinned at his question. I was not offended, though I should have been. I just thought that it was so *outré*, yet so expected, from an insular, intimate and boundary-crossing synagogue *habitué*.

"It doesn't matter," I answered. "It's always painful, especially when children are involved."

"My sister got a divorce and she has never been so happy."

Strike Two. Gossiping about his sister.

Strike Three was not far behind. He began to tell tales about the former rabbi of the synagogue.

"Ssh!" I said, putting my index finger to my lips.

"Why?"

Despite his bluntness bordering on rudeness, I could not help but be amused at the self-possessiveness of this prankster.

"The cantor was very good," I said to the *schul* historian.

"Would you like to meet him?

"Yes," I answered and stood up.

"He does stand-up comedy."

"He does?"

"Yes."

"Is he any good?"

"You'll have to ask him."

I introduced myself to the cantor.

"You have a beautiful voice," I said.

"Thank you," he said, smiling.

"You do stand-up?"

"Yes."

"Where?"

"Ships, theaters."

Somehow, I could not reconcile this man, this trained advocate of prayer, this deliverer of holy tunes, standing in front of a raucous, half-drunk crowd.

"Did you go to yeshiva?"

"No," he said shaking his head.

"Well, you are very good."

"Thanks."

He turned to talk to his companion.

I turned to leave but someone directed me to the tall, grey haired man who had made the announcements during the service. His unusual name sounded familiar and then I realized who he was.

His family had owned and operated a famous kosher restaurant on the Lower East Side. His brother had been killed in an unsolved robbery as he was on his way to the bank to deposit the restaurant's receipts.

"My father knew your brother," I said. "He said that he was very kindhearted and generous and that he used to feed poor people for free."

"Thank you," the man said.

"My father was also a Holocaust survivor, like your brother. They were both in Siberia. Where is the restaurant now?"

"We have two."

"Do you still have the Chinese waitresses?"

"Yes. They still think they are Jewish."

"Do you still work in the restaurant?"

"No, I've retired."

"Completely?"

"Yes."

"Well, I will be sure to go in if I am in the area. Good *Shabbos*."

"Good *Shabbos*."

When I returned to my son's apartment, he was awake and making coffee.

"You really should go," I said. "You haven't found a *schul* in all these years."

"Yeah."

"Well, at least go during the week. They have jazz nights."

"I'll think about it."

"What do you want to do today?" I asked.

"I don't know," he mumbled.

"I'd like to visit the grave of the Lubavitcher Rebbe before I leave. He's somewhere in Queens."

"No, thanks."

"How about the Met?"

"Ugh."

The day wore on.

Somehow, cajoling, guilt inducing, demanding, maneuvering, I managed to get myself, my son and daughter and my cousin and her daughter, who had driven in from Bayside, to the Metropolitan Museum.

I directed my cousin towards the Roman Gallery. I wanted to visit Hercules. He stood on a pedestal, imperious, full bearded, muscular, handsome, a lion skin wrapped about his shoulders, its paws on falling on his pectoral muscles.

I waved at him. The security guard, standing beside him, waved back.

"Not you," I said. "Him."

I entered the Greek Hall, searching for the Praxiteles statue of the teenage Aphrodite. I circled it slowly. Its modesty and eroticism was breathtaking.

We sped towards the Egyptian Division. There it was. The yellow jasper fragment of a woman's head. Its porcelain-like surface reflected the overhead lights. Its curved lip suggested a bountiful sensuousness. If it had not been damaged, lost, it would have rivaled the head of Nefertiti in the Berlin Museum.

I sighed with relief. I had seen my favorites.

I went back to Bayside, leaving my daughter to stay with my son.

The following day, we looked at family photos as we waited for the arrival of the daughter of our mothers' eldest sister.

Soon, she walked into the room.

"I want to visit the tomb of the Rebbe," she announced. "My mother is right near there," she added. "I want to visit her, too."

"So do I," I said.

"You're not going like that!" she announced, pointing to my shorts and sleeveless shirt.

"Are you crazy?" my younger cousin demanded. "Don't you think she knows what to wear?"

I stepped into the fray.

"Hold it," I said. "I know how to dress. Do you have a skirt I could borrow?"

We rooted around in my cousin's closet and she gave me a long, narrow, black skirt.

"It looks good. Keep it," she said.

We drove towards the cemetery.

Speeding past a sign that read 'EXIT. NO ENTRY', my younger cousin drove onto the property.

"What are you doing?" screamed my older cousin.

"I always go this way," she said.

We passed a funeral, parked cars, and groups of wandering visitors, flowers in hand.

We drove aimlessly up and down the narrow roads with cheery, bucolic names. My cousins continued to bicker, instructing each other as to my aunt's location.

Finally we reached the farthest corner of the grounds. There was nowhere else to go.

"This is it," one of them said.

I stepped out of the car and began to walk in the direction they had indicated and hobbled by the skirt, promptly fell headfirst to the ground.

The sound of my skull hitting the asphalt sounded like a thunderclap and I was certain I was dead.

My cousins shrieked and came running.

"Sit down," they insisted as I struggled to rise.

"I'm all right," I said, strangely feeling no pain.

"Wow. It looked like someone knocked you down," my younger cousin said.

They helped me rise and sat me down on a tilted concrete bench.

Someone gave me a frozen bottle of water to hold to my head.

"I'm fine," I said, somewhat incredulously as I had fully expected my head to be fractured.

"Wait a minute."

"Okay," I said.

After a while, I rose, and began to walk towards the grave.

I stared straight ahead, unbelievingly.

"You spelled her name wrong," I told my cousin.

There, in all its engraved glory was my aunt's name written as "Frieda".

"But that's the way she spelled it on her papers."

"I know how she spelled it. She told me."

"Well, maybe she spelled it both ways."

"And you have the date of birth wrong. She was eleven years old than my mother."

"What?"

"Maybe she made herself older," my younger cousin volunteered.

"Why?"

"For social security."

"And you spelled "Holocaust" wrong. Twice."

"Where?"

"It's 'Holocaust' not "Holocost"".

The three of us stared at the tombstone.

"Didn't anyone ever say anything? In thirteen years?"

They remained silent.

A black and white electroplated image of my aunt and her husband, hung from the marker. I remembered her thick wig and my uncle's jaunty Alpine hat, perched sideways, covering the same part of his skull that I had just struck. They both were smiling broadly.

We stayed a while and then I kissed my fingers and placed them on the side of her marker.

"I get it," I whispered and smiled.

Somewhere in *Gan Eden,* my aunt was laughing.

We re-entered the car.

"I hurt my shoulder," I said, lowering my sweater. The skin was scraped and a bruise was starting to swell.

We drove to the cemetery where the Rebbe was buried.

His resting place was located at the border of the enclosure. Entry was accessible at all times from the street.

In order to visit, one entered through a building which contained a prayer room, rows of benches and desks equipped with pens and papers, a library and a room with a continuous video loop of a *fabringenen* of the Rebbe and other Hasidim.

I sat down and began to write a note.

Suddenly, all about me was silent.

My cousins looked at me expectantly.

I started to write.

"Dear Rebbe," I began. "You know what happened."

I wrote and wrote.

I wrote my father's name.

I sped on. I wrote the names of my children.

I wrote, grateful for the opportunity to tell the Rebbe, assured that he was listening.

Hot tears rolled out from under my sunglasses, down my cheeks.

We lit candles in another room, then entered the grave site.

The Rebbe and his father-in-law, the previous Rebbe were side by side.

Thousands of pieces of white paper fluttered on their graves.

I saw young men, wearing black jackets and jeans, deep in prayer standing around the enclosure.

A little girl, not more than five, in eloquent Yiddish, told a man, "It's not very big, Daddy, but it's very nice."

I placed my message on the grave.

"My shoulder stopped hurting!" I exclaimed as we walked to the car.

My older cousin nodded. My other cousin said nothing.

On our first Sabbath back in Palm Beach, I rushed to attend services.

After fruitlessly trying to persuade my somnambulant daughter to accompany me, I went alone.

As I opened the tall doors to the sanctuary, I heard the familiar voice of my rabbi, announcing the fourth *aliya,* or calling the fourth person up to bless the torah.

I winced. I was late.

"This chapter is about the conclusion of the Jews sojourn in the desert," he said.

I took my seat.

THE WEDDING MARCH

My daughter and I watched the wedding planner.

A few minutes earlier, seconds before we were to enter the chamber where the ceremony was to take place, a fire alarm went off and a recorded female voice ordered us to evacuate (her word) the building.

I refused to budge.

I thought, "I am not hearing this."

The warning was repeated.

She finally walked away, holding the train of her wedding gown in her hand.

Although I had promised myself that I would not think of it, all the years of single parenthood flashed before my eyes. The graduations. The awards. Her first car. College. Engagement.

She was a child of my later years, fulfilling a desire to have another child, a daughter.

She was a beautiful infant (silken white hair, black eyes, button nose) but she was never as they say "cuddly".

When she was born, she emitted such a high pitched sound that I wondered if they could hear her at the hospital across town.

As she grew, she screamed a lot. Loudly.

She would refuse to let me put her down. She demanded that I carry her everywhere.

I used to tell observers, weakly "Someday you will pay to hear her in the Metropolitan Opera House."

I never tried to rein her in.

I admired her verve, her confidence, her ability to assert herself.

In the years to come, I came to realize that that the force of her will in turn, would strengthen and reinforce me as well.

As we waited outside the hall, the voice once again insisted that we abandon the premises.

I remained motionless.

I continued to hold my left elbow bent as if to support her (nonexistent) arm.

The groom's uncle came running out and told me he was going to call security.

It didn't matter.

I remained in place.

I wondered where my daughter had gone.

I looked around.

I saw her walk into the bride's preparation room, chatting calmly with the planner. Her long, honey blonde hair shone under the overhead lights. She moved gracefully and determinedly.

Finally, the uncle came back and said that there had been a kitchen fire, it had been contained and that we were to proceed.

My daughter returned and we walked forward, side by side, in step.

www.ingramcontent.com/pod-product-compliance
Lightning Source LLC
Chambersburg PA
CBHW020339160726
47992CB00004B/1893